Maestro

Melissa Rea

Maestro was a labor of love with the help of many. First I want to thank Sally Stotts, who first loved the story of my Gabriella. Thank you to Barb Rogan for all your help taking a good story to a readable novel. Thank you for all my friends who read various drafts and gave me their opinions. Last but not least I want to thank Gabrielle Giffords who was shot on the day I began my story and inspired me to name my heroine after a woman lovely, smart and strong enough to survive a bullet to her head. Now that's a heroine.

CHAPTER ONE

I stand this bright summer morning on the gallows that will end my life. Though the sun rises just above the trees and warms my face, my whole body trembles. I feel a soft breeze ruffle my hair and plaster it to the tears that flow down my cheeks. I rub my wrists, grateful that the soldiers who guard me feel I no longer need to be tied. They stand twenty feet from me, looking bored, evidently unafraid that I might escape. A high wall encloses the courtyard surrounding the gallows. Down a narrow street, I see several buildings and red liveried soldiers stand at this entrance as well. Three people stand watching: a milkmaid, a young blacksmith and a dwarf.

It is odd that this gallows stands within the walls of a convent, close to Venice, where I spent so much happy time. A nun told me, as she watched me dress in this simple white garment that will be my last, that this gallows is reserved for the execution of important people in special circumstances. Am I special because I am innocent of any murder? Or is this a parting gift from friends who, though they cannot stop my death, have arranged this special place for my execution?

This singular gallows looks more like a stage than a place to end one's life. The wood I stand upon is over twenty feet wide and the boards have been sanded and feel smooth as silk beneath my bare feet. The dark wood from which the rope will hang is polished with wax until it gleams in the morning light. Though the setting may be special, the play to be performed today can only be a tragedy.

I catch my breath and feel the need to speak to those souls who will witness my end. "I beg of you your kindness. Would one of you have something I might sit upon?"

The woman takes a step nearer, pushes a dubiously white cap back on her head with a plump hand and answers me. "I'll not lift my little pinky to give no murderess comfort. Them you killed ain't none too comfortable, I'd wager. Them that rots stinking in the grave." The woman bites off those words through thin pale lips and rubs her hands against her ragged dress, splashed from hem to sleeve with mud. She hugs a milking pail tight against her.

I smile as best I can manage. "Your point is a good one and you would win that wager, but I am innocent. The girl I stand accused of murdering was my friend, and I grieve for her death as much as for my own, too soon to come. Though I will hang for her murder, my only crime is that I tried to save her."

Tomorrow would mark the beginning of my nineteenth year. I fear there is little chance I will see that day dawn. I find it ever more difficult to stem the tide of tears.

The woman cackles and nods at the two men standing near her. "Ain't none of our concern why you swing. And that sniveling won't change a thing." She pushes the tangle of red hair that hangs below her cap out of her eyes and she looks me up and down as if I were a cow whose milk has soured. Smirking, she turns her milk pail over and sits down. "We come to watch a hanging and watch it we will."

She speaks true. I must pass the short time left me with some bit of grace, as I was taught. Perhaps if I could tell my tale, their listening might give me a crumb of comfort. I can do nothing but sit awkwardly on the edge of the gallows and tug the thin garment up at the neck in an attempt at modesty. I look at the three people staring up at me in anticipation of the entertainment I will soon provide. "Might it be more pleasant to hear my tale than to watch me snivel?"

They examine me, squinting in the morning light. The young blacksmith in a leather apron smiles at me. "I will listen, Miss. I want to know your tale." His face is smudged with soot, but his dark eyes are kind. He stands tall, muscled arms crossed. The tiny man between the milkmaid and the blacksmith is dressed all in brown and holds a pitchfork. On his back is a pack nearly as large as he. He says nothing but nods and in his smile there are fewer teeth than in his fork. He lays his fork on the ground and settles down on his pack to listen. The young man stands with his feet wide apart. Shifting her weight until she is comfortable on the overturned bucket, the woman looks up at me expectantly.

I begin.

"My life, short that it may be, has not been all sorrow, and I would tell the good with the bad."

"Wait," says the young man in the leather apron. "I will fetch you my stool. I'll do no blacksmithing till this deed be done, anyway." He runs across the courtyard and down the street a short way to a rough wood building with smoke curling out of a brick chimney. Returning in a few minutes with arms full, he hands me a three-legged stool, then sits himself down on a nail keg.

The milkmaid snorts. "You, Smithy, I wager you'd not be giving her a thing if she weren't a pretty piece. Everybody knows what brings any of you with a prick to stiffen at the sight. That thin dress they gives 'em for hanging don't cover much." The woman cocks her head at me. "That angel's face won't keep you from swingin' but go on. My milkin's done for the morning and I got nothin' better to do." She leans back and begins to pick her teeth with a piece of straw.

Now sitting comfortably on the blacksmith's stool, I begin again.

"My name is Maria Gabriella Constanzi, daughter to the Count Pompeii of Florence. I inherited this face from my dear mother. It has served me well, as such things can be of use to a maid." I could feel my cheeks grow hot; but if I am to tell my story, I must tell all of it and tell it true.

"You can believe what I tell you, for what would be the point of lies on my last day? I beg your indulgence when I call myself a maid, because while I have no husband, neither have I the innocence to deserve that title. Thank you, gentle lady and kind gentlemen, for agreeing to listen." I give my audience a little bow of my head even on the gallows I cannot shed the manners taught me by my mother.

The smithy gestures toward the milkmaid. "Bess surely ain't no lady."

The red head cuffs him in the ear. "Marco, you ain't no gentleman, nor Spud neither."

We all laugh. Even in this most dire of circumstances, this shared laughter soothes me.

CHAPTER TWO

I'm told I was born on the warmest day of high summer in the last year of the century, 1699, to the Count and Countess Pompeii. My mother was considered quite old to give birth, and my father was even older.

At thirty-five years, my mother was overjoyed to have finally delivered a child. I was told that the fateful summer day I pushed out of my mother's womb was hailed with unequaled celebration. My Noble parents had been married for many years without issue. My birth quelled the fear there would be no heir to the Pompeii estate.

After my birth, my proud parents never referred to me as their daughter, but rather as the Pompeii heir. My sex did not affect the abundance of their love nor the lavishness of my upbringing.

Bess shifts on her bucket and addresses me. "Don't miss the plums and sausage one bit, does you, girl? I've always managed fine without 'em."

I laugh. "Every milestone of any import in my life was celebrated with jubilant feasts and the lavish gifts of alms to the poor. My first steps fed the villagers for days. After my fifth birthday, no beggar child heard his stomach growl for a month.

Because I was educated as a noble heir rather than a mere female, I learned to read, write and use weapons appropriate to my noble stature. Any subject in which I showed the slightest interest brought the best tutors available in all of Florence to our gate.

On the anniversary of my sixth year, the usual feast was accompanied by many musicians playing all manner of music. Though I'd heard music before, on this day I sat spellbound before an assemblage of the best musicians playing instruments of which I had never even dreamed. I marveled at the harpsichord's notes as I watched the young musician's fingers fly over the keyboard. The lovely sounds from the hautboy made me smile from ear to ear, and the violin soloist brought tears to my eyes.

The next day, the very best music teachers were hired from Florence, Venice, and even one from Vienna: six new teachers who gave me as much time as I desired each day. I learned that the music was written in notes. I learned to read these notes, and not merely copy the sounds I heard. I practiced the harpsichord and other instruments for hours on end. My mother would come to hear my progress and always sat smiling at my little concerts. I am told that I was often found slumped over the harpsichord, fast asleep.

One day, I heard my teachers talking among themselves. They did not know I was listening. I had hidden behind the thick drapes in the music room as I often did, hoping to hear things they would not say to me.

"And we're supposed to believe a thing you say?" Bess cries in disgust. "Spying on your elders, giving away your maidenhead. If you didn't look so much like an angel with your gold curls and your big green eyes, nobody would listen to a word."

The little man is on his feet, scowling, drawing his hand across his mouth as if to silence her.

"Here now, Bess," says Marco, the blacksmith. "Shut your cake hole. She's got a story to tell and we've nothing better to do." They settle down, and I continue.

"The first to speak was Giacomo, the laziest of my music teachers. "It ain't natural the way that child plays. I'm tempted to choke the life from the demanding little she-devil."

From my hiding place I glimpsed Adolfo, the kindest and the

wisest of my teachers, sitting on the harpsichord bench, resting his grey head in his hands. He sat up and spoke sharply to Giacomo. "Touching that child would be a most grievous crime, you pig of a lout. The world would lose an exceptional talent, and you would lose your worthless flea's nest of a head." Rage swelling, he stood and pointed a bony finger at Giacomo, "If you are not up to it, I am sure a more patient and certainly more worthy recorder teacher can be found. No doubt the Count would prefer one who does not eat so much."

"The child hears the notes in her head, just by sight!" Giacomo whispered, "It is not natural for one so young."

"It is the sign of exceptional talent, not the devil. Make yourself useful and help me choose music for her concert."

Giacomo would not be silenced. "Whoever heard of a child of seven giving a concert? Talented or not, the child is ruinously spoiled. And I'm telling you: it is not at all a natural thing, this skill of hers." He crossed himself with his thick fingers.

And then I laughed, giving away my presence, but I could not contain my happiness. I ran out from behind the curtains to Adolfo.

"Am I really to give a concert, Adolfo?"

His soft brown eyes looked upon me with patience and kindness, that day and always. "Yes, Gabriella. Your mother wishes it to be."

"When? When will this be?" I jumped up and down, pulling on his sleeve.

Adolfo patted my head. "We must get you ready, my dear girl. It will take time and a great deal of practice. Perhaps in a few months."

I shook my head. "If we leave off sleeping so much and eat only once each day, I could be ready in a week. I am a big girl now and I can reach almost all the notes on the harpsichord. Oh please let me play the harpsichord at my concert!" Giacomo slapped his forehead. "God have mercy on us all if she were not the devil's own spawn!"

Three weeks later, my concert took place.

I remember so clearly the look on the faces of all assembled as

I walked to the harpsichord, that glorious morning. My beaming parents, our entire household and those of several neighboring estates were seated in chairs, arranged in rows in the largest banquet hall. Crossing the room to my harpsichord, I looked only at the gleaming wood of the floor. Part of me wanted to run and hide in the shelter of the drapes, but I held my head high.

I knew they saw me as just a pretty little girl in the white lace dress with pink ribbons tied in her golden hair. But when I finished my hour's harpsichord performance, there was only silence. I looked at the assembly and saw every mouth hanging open in surprise. Tears glistened on cheeks. A moment later the room burst into enthusiastic applause. I was quite used to the praise given a pretty and privileged child, but this was different—this was for my performance. I felt as if my heart would burst.

Thus music became my joy, my salvation, and the lovely road that led me to this gallows.

CHAPTER THREE

My musical exploration and the whole of my elaborate education continued until the fall of my twelfth year. The pleasure of my spoiled and perfect existence ended with two catastrophic turns. First, my beloved mother fell terribly ill.

"Why, Papa, is Mother so pale and weak?" I asked. "She eats nothing and still her belly swells.'"

"Her physician is not sure." He held me tight and smoothed my hair. There were tears in his dark eyes. "If she were younger they might think her with child but..." He shook his head sadly. Surely this is not possible, I thought.

Oh, my dearest and certainly final friends, it was indeed possible. They came into the world one week before my thirteenth birthday: Roberto Vincenza Italo and Ricardo Juliano Giacomo, two perfect baby boys who ruined my life.

Spud jumps up and down clapping. Marco speaks calmly quietly in the tiny man's ear, "Them babies ain't a good thing, Spud. She said they ruined her life."

Spud's smile fades.

Bess looks annoyed. The crowd has grown. Now talking and laughing, but Bess, Marco and Spud give Gabriella their rapt attention. More people now stand in a second row, and a third begins to form. The newcomers frivolity is the usual accompaniment for an execution.

Bess rises off her bucket with a groan. "If you can't keep your mouths shut so she can tell her story, then you best be gone." The look on her face is dark as summer storm. She dares anyone to say a word with that look. The newcomers grow silent and move closer to listen.

"Did I say ruined my life? It was ruin as Vesuvius wrought on the city of my family's name, or so I thought at thirteen. It was as if I no longer existed. The miraculous birth of twin male heirs erased my existence as the volcano erased the city of Pompeii, I thought at the time. I could have been covered in a four-inch layer of ash for all the notice I now received. Was I not still the image of my beautiful mother? Did not my playing wring tears from all who listened? It mattered little.

I was now merely a female child, to be raised to an age to be married to the most advantageous Noble house. My mother and father still smiled when I came to see them, but only briefly, having little time for me. The light once shined so brightly upon me was now dimmed. It focused completely on Roberto and Ricardo.

My birthday was nearly forgotten that year. The trained animals and numerous performers that usually came for the celebration, did not appear. There were no pretty ponies with monkey jockeys to make me laugh. I was moved to a smaller chamber on the north side of our house. Perhaps I should have noticed it was the loveliest of all the rooms in our home, with a large round turret that overlooked the flower garden; but my pain and jealousy would not let me see its beauty.

All my instruments were moved to a large room next door and a door created between. Still I felt only the pain of my replacements' birth. The beautiful new tapestries and new rich red and gold carpets did little to soothe my hurt. I sulked in self-pity, sitting on the lavender silk coverlet of my bed under the matching canopy.

Half my staff of teachers had been dismissed. The twin gods being still in swaddling, they required only nurses. I was allowed to keep my Adolfo, a Greek and Latin teacher, and a riding instructor.

One day, my mother tore herself away from my brothers and came to speak to me. "I think, my precious, that you should be allowed to ride now. Riding is a useful skill for a single lady in search of a suitable husband."

I could not bear to meet her gaze but continued to bang my harpsichord keyboard without mercy. At last I stopped and spoke without looking at her. "This lady had no such interest or desire to be married."

I was all of fourteen.

"Someday you will change your mind, my love." She reached over and lifted my chin looking into my eyes with her own, their mirror image. Her golden curls, only lightly streaked with silver, still gleamed.

Though I had no need of a husband, I was happy to be allowed to ride. Would that my mother had forbade it! Riding brought me joy and freedom, but it would lead me to a most ruinous passion.

I was now allowed unlimited access, not only to the stables, but to my father's extensive library. It was one of the Pompeii estate's greatest assets; there was not another like it anywhere, even in Florence. My Latin was excellent and my Greek passable. I was allowed to browse alone among the stacks covering all four of the long walls, floor to ceiling. I spent hours sprawled on the thick blue carpet or in my father's favorite green velvet chair, poring over the pages.

My family's fortune came from velvets, I learned sitting at my father's knee in that library as he explained the way the world worked. "We have the finest textile design manufactory in this part of the world," he told me with great pride. "We purchase all manner of velvets in their raw state, cheaply. Then, our workers embellish them with gold and silver threads as well as pearls and even precious gems for those that can afford them. The demand for this fine work has been high of late and our profits are generous. Thank goodness as your music teachers alone would break a man of less means." Though I knew he was teasing me, I looked peeved until he burst out laughing and wrapped me in his strong arms.

Nevertheless, my life grew colder and much less brilliant in keeping with my new station, the mere daughter of the Count. It seemed unfair that my lack of one simple appendage could cause such a drastic demotion.

"I got what you need right here, girl," calls a skinny, dark-haired man in the gathering crowd. Bess gives him her murderous look. Others in the groups murmur threats. He is quiet and I continue.

Each day my brothers grew larger, stronger and brighter. I might have wished them dead, but that would have been evil. Despite my imminent execution, I am a good girl, as I hope to convince you, and perhaps remind myself, before I leave this earth. I'll admit I tried to hate my little brothers, but I could not. They were so beautiful and so innocent. Ricardo looked just like mother and me, with the same luscious white curls that would turn to gold as he grew. Roberto had black hair and dark brown eyes and was the image of our father. I could only love the little instruments of my replacement, though I could not help but wonder what they had that made them so much more precious. Curiosity is my most ruinous fault, as you will see.

The little heirs were rarely left alone. A team of nurses watched over them everywhere, lest any harm befall the Count's long-awaited sons. I wanted to examine them for myself, and I watched for my opportunity. One morning I marveled to find little Ricardo alone in his crib, pulling on his toes and laughing. I knew that this might be my only chance. I crept up to the cradle covered with golden angels and inlaid with ivory stars. Slowly and carefully I unwrapped the damp and smelly linen around his little pink body. This required a good deal of effort. His smile put his cradle's carved cherubs to shame. Ricardo was the most sweet-natured of the twins. I felt lucky to have found him alone and not his brother. Roberto might have fussed and I would have been discovered. At last I removed the cloth around him, and there it was. There, where his legs joined. was a tiny pinkish purple bit of flesh. It was half as long as my little finger and looked for all the world like any noodle to be served with tomato sauce. Below was a larger wrinkled ball of flesh was what looked like my thumb when in the bath too long. Nothing all remarkable, it seemed to me.

Just as I picked up the smelly cloth to wrap my brother's tiny blessing the way I'd found it, a stream hit me in my eye. I screamed, Ricardo laughed, and the nurses rushed in.

"It's just a little piss, Miss. Not likely to kill ye. That is what baby boys does." Marta was the oldest and wisest of the noble nurses. She laughed at my screaming until she had no more breath.

"Make it stop!" I cried. Ricardo continued both pissing and laughing.

The second nurse spoke. "Oh there's no stop'n him until he's done. It's as right as any nature's rain," She struggled to contain her own laughter by covering her mouth with her hand. Ricardo continued pissing as five nurses quickly gathered round the crib to insure his safety.

Ricardo became my least favorite brother. I did not make the mistake of unwrapping him again.

Having seen his tiny appendage, I was more mystified than ever as to why people placed any value on such a thing.

CHAPTER FOUR

On my fourteenth birthday, an enormous crate arrived. Four men carried into my music room. It took forever to uncrate. When all the boards were pried off, I could not comprehend what I saw. The instrument had a keyboard like my harpsichord, but this keyboard was attached to a huge upright triangular wooden box reaching nearly three feet above the keyboard. The wood was decorated with painted vines and flowers. It was huge compared to any such harpsichord I had ever seen. I reached out to touch one key, and the sound that rang out took my breath away. While each note on my harpsichord tinkled like the small bells rang at mass, this note rang out loud and glorious, like the bells in the church tower. This, I was told by Adolpho, was a magnificent pianoforte. "It is a new instrument and very few exist. A man named Cristofel has invented this wonder, and your father ordered one for you."

One of the men who delivered my magnificent gift stood watching and seemed amused at my delight. His jacket was trimmed in velvet and he lingered as the others returned to the wagon, bending over to polish the road dust from the keys. "I am glad you are to play her," he said to me. "Her beauty deserves to be enjoyed by one such as you."

"Thank you, Sir. Can you tell me how the sound is produced that it is so much richer than any harpsichord?" I pulled the bench from my harpsichord and placed it in front of the pianoforte.

The man walked around to the back and opened a hinged cover, revealing long wire strings as if part of a triangular harp. "The strings of the pianoforte are much longer and are struck by hammers rather than plucked as in the harpsichord. The resulting sound is unique. Will you play? I would like to make certain the road has not done her any harm." He watched with his arms crossed as I lay my hands on the lovely keys. I played a little piece I loved and knew from memory. When I stopped, he pulled a wooden instrument from his pocket, opened the cover and turned a little wooden screw that tightened one string a tiny bit. Handing me the little wooden key, he said, "She is yours now."

My fingers struck the keys once more and the strong bright notes that rang forth filled the room with glory. I hardly did this grand instrument justice, but the look on the man's face assured me he was satisfied with the sound. Without another word, he gave me a little bow and left.

Was this Cristofel himself? I never knew for certain, but the look of paternal pride on the man's face led me to suspect it.

Adolfo watched me play with wonder on his care-worn face, running his hands over the upright sounding box as if caressing a lover. The notes soon flew from the paper to my fingers and filled the air with their power and their abundance. Though the keyboard was similar, the sound eclipsed that of my little harpsichord. The pianoforte was played so much like a harpsichord, I had little trouble learning this new and wondrous instrument.

Along with my beloved pianoforte, I was fascinated by the recorder and spent a large amount of time coaxing sweet notes from it. The hautboy filled the air with deep and magical notes after some practice. It was the soft, sweet and terrible violin alone that vexed me.

"Adolfo, what is wrong with me?" I asked my teacher one afternoon. I cannot make the violin notes anything but sour and scratchy."

"When a pure note is played on a violin, few sounds

compare, I agree Gabriella. The violin is not an instrument, but an obsession. Your harpsichord and soon your pianoforte are better than any student I have yet heard. Leave some talent for others."

"'I will not have this!'" I stomped my foot and redoubled my efforts, practicing the flesh nearly off of my fingers. Still the notes would scratch and squeak far too often, and when they did not, they were merely adequate.

I could not give up. The most beautiful compositions were written for that demon instrument. A tiny misplacement of my finger would result in an imperfect note which ruined the performance. I managed to console myself with lovely piano pieces and the occasional long intricate recorder sonata.

The years passed. I grew taller and more pleasingly made with each year. I say this without pretense of humility, in the shadow of the gallows.

"I'll agree with that," Marco calls, and Spud nods. Another man reaches out his hands and licks his lips in a suggestive way. The crowd laughs. I blush and Bess gives her fiercest look at the assembled rowdies. They fall silent. I continue.

It would have been better if I had grown a hump on my back and a wart on my nose. Then I might not be standing on this gallows. Alas, I was near as tall as my father, and the bosom appearing above my gowns garnered appropriate attention. My time was now split between the music room, riding stable, and the library. Most mornings began with a trip to the stable. The freedom I felt when mounted on the back of my white palfrey took away the pain of my replacement a little.

My riding teacher was old and lazy. When it was clear I needed no more lessons, he slept while I rode off alone. This arrangement benefitted us both. I enjoyed my liberty, and he was paid, housed, and fed for doing almost nothing. My time at the stables taught me more than any tutors. Much could be learned by observing the animals. All manner of life passed before me in the stables and corrals. I watched the animals mate, give birth, and even die. This cycle of life took place every day within the livestock compound. Once I held a newborn calf in my arms and watched the life drain from its mother's soft brown eyes into a deep red puddle in the stall.

The stable boys were always glad to answer my questions. The more I grew, the more stable boys and field hands I had at my beck and call. I took great delight in watching them work and informed them how they could do their jobs more efficiently, as if I knew. My bossiness became legendary.

A voice calls from the third row of audience, "Aint bossin' nobody now are you, girl?" The crowd, ever larger now, joins in their laughter. I turn to look back at the wooden scaffold where soon my life will end. I study it in silence for a moment, but the crowd begs for more.

My musical education progressed so well that Adolfo had trouble keeping me in music I had not already mastered. Certainly I lived no Spartan's life. I had music from far and wide. I enjoyed George Phillipe Telemann as well as any and often wore my teacher out with many a long and tedious concerts. Tedious for him, I mean, as I would sooner play than breathe back then. Lovely Italian composers held my attention for many a long while. There was Thomaso Albinoni, whose work was magnificent, though sometimes very sad. "Albanoni is a strange quiet little man," Adolfo said, as he sat tuning my harpsichord. "I do not think you would like him, Gabriella."

"Oh, I am sure I would love him as I love the beautiful music he creates. Why can you not get me more of his work? No more violin, though. It just makes my fingers hurt and I want to scream and throw it out the window."

Adolfo smiled his kind and patient smile. "Senore Albibnoni is said to have such significant wealth that he does not seek patrons. It is difficult to get him to turn loose of his compositions. I heard a rumor that the adagio you love so much was written after he lost the love of his life."

· · ·

Music was my life then. I would fall asleep with notes scrolling across my eyelids and echoing in my ears, an innocent bliss that was soon to end.

One morning, Adolfo brought me a most marvelous gift. For my fifteenth birthday, my parents had sent him to a large music dealer in Venice. He returned with an entire cart full of sheets of music. This gift seemed at that moment all I could ever want. My mother was busy with the boys, now two years old and twice the bother. It touched me deeply to know she loved me enough to give me my heart's desire—what was then my heart's desire.

As I pored through new music, I marveled at the beauty and the variety. There were, of course, Germans whose works were new to me and lovely, if not always too terribly challenging. There were several interesting Venetians, most of them familiar. As I sorted through the glorious pages, one amazing piece sent me to running to my keyboard at the mere sight. I could not wait to play it. It was such a wonder, light, happy and infinitely challenging. The fast-slow-fast movements held me rapt before I touched a key. I loved the ritornello style of it. I would have played all night were I not ordered to stop so Ricardo and Roberto could sleep. I actually felt a great sadness when I finally put down the sheets signed at the bottom, "Antonio Vivaldi" and fell asleep smiling.

Music always thrilled me, but at fifteen a paper lover would not long satisfy.

"Because no girl lives on music alone," someone far back in the crowd yells. I know too well the truth of those words, but I wait for the hoots and laughter to die down again before I continue. My spirit soared at the pleasure of holding my audience's attention and pleasing them.

I often went to the stables. Some days I actually rode, but most days were merely for observation. One such day, my mission became much sweeter or darker, I know not exactly which. I'd watched the stable boys work and grow for years. They'd all changed before my eyes from pudgy or scrawny boys with dirty hair and dirtier nails into men. Most were quite ordinary. Antonio was not.

He was the Greek god Apollo I saw once in a book. His deep dark eyes seemed the very eyes that looked down at me from the paintings of angels in church. He wore his blue-black hair much longer than was the fashion, and the curls that caressed his broad shoulders made him look even more like a painting of an angel. I would pretend to groom my white palfrey Lillia and stand, curry comb in hand, drinking in the sight of him.

"I would have gladly taught you to ride, girl...and would have ridden you into the ground," says a nasty-looking man from near the back of the growing crowd. His filthy cloth apron is covered with dark stains and he is missing an eye. A man beside him punches him in the stomach. A tussle breaks out.

Bess stands with legs apart and raises her voice above the fray. "Quiet, you oafs! I'll box your ears proper if you don't pipe down." Her fists were raised and her look fierce. "The next one of you louts that says one word gets this bucket thrown at his head. This is the last time I warns you. Marco here can take any man jack of you." Marco nods and Spud attempts a stern look with crossed arms and his hat low on his brow.

Never doubting Bess's word, the crowd falls quiet.

I learned, through watching, when it was time for Antonio to clean the stalls. It was a dirty job, and the boys who did it wore next to nothing, as whatever was worn would never be the same again.

One glorious afternoon, I was brushing my palfrey when I spotted Antonio leaning on a shovel, shirtless, with his back to me. The thin britches he wore were rolled up at the bottom and down at the waist and they were soaked with sweat. I felt the breath catch in my throat and my heart pound. His black hair glistened, and sweat ran down his tanned back, chiseled like the marble statue I had seen in Florence. But Antonio had been carved by hard work alone. When he turned around, I saw his chest, damp, rippling with muscles as he moved. A little trail of dark hair curled around and headed southward growing thicker until it disappeared into the folds of his damp work britches. As my eyes traced this trail I felt a strange and foreign feeling in a place between my legs.

This was new to me, this strange longing. Antonio gazed directly back at me, as if he knew of my discovery and was not at all displeased. My face flushed with embarrassment, but the strange feeling clearly became hunger. On his face this time was a smirk, as if he knew this, too.

"I am surprised," said Antonio, "you have not yet brushed the hair completely off that palfrey." The sound of his voice, rich and low, washed over me and I shivered as if on the coldest day.

I gathered what remained of my dignity. "I have finished my job, but you have quite a lot of work left to you. I would use the larger square shovel to do the job more effectively, if I were you."

"Oh, yes? And is shoveling horse shit work you have done often?"

"Well, no, but it seems to me..." I stopped. He'd moved closer and suddenly it was hard to breathe. He smelled of manure and sweat and something...wholly Antonio.

His smile widened. "You can help me if you wish." Cheeks burning, I ran to put Lillia in her stall. He called after me: "Come back, little chicken. I will lend you some britches, and you can use the big square shovel."

I ran back to the house with all the speed I could manage and hurried to my music room.

I picked up my violin, a feeble attempt to rid my body of this feeling. Choosing the most difficult concerto, I butchered it without mercy for hours. Practice was not everything, as the violin had taught me. The magical connection between instrument and player was lacking, though I played until my fingers bled. And after all that, the hunger remained, like an itch I could not scratch. I lay awake for hours, thinking. There was only one remedy for what ailed me: Antonio.

CHAPTER FIVE

I knew very little of him, the source of my anguish. He was not born on the Pompeii Estate, I heard someone say. He must have received some education, as the words rolled off his tongue with an elegance none of the other stable boys could match. He always wore a smirk and rarely a shirt. His handsome lips turned up at the corner and for some reason, he often smiled out of just one side. As for his lack of a shirt, I reasoned that perhaps he dressed for the heat, but I venture to guess he enjoyed the female attention his shirtless state most certainly attracted. There was nearly always some girl from the house or kitchen, cheeks freshly scrubbed and pinched to heighten color, bringing him lunch or dinner. They would hang on the fence or stand outside the stalls, making conversation long after the food had grown cold. I watched with a jealous and disapproving eye, but Antonio did not seem to mind them.

I did not understand this strange feeling I had, but I would not approach Antonio without some idea of what I wanted from him. It seems so silly and so innocent now; but I would not have those dark eyes of his look upon me again with only amusement.

Stolen glimpses of Antonio served only to increase my itch. My nights grew ever more restless and unsatisfying. I desperately needed advice. There was something wrong with me and I needed to set it right.

But from whom could I seek help? Often I listened as the chamber maids made their morning rounds. This had yielded valuable information in the past, but not this time. Both were much older than me, and I dared not ask. I had no older sister or close friend to turn to, and it would be unseemly to ask my mother. In the past, such physical questions could have been addressed to my nurse, but she left years ago, sent on to cousins in Naples.

The maids or kitchen girls would have to do, I decided at last. I studied them.

I made a study after supper one evening, and I chose Anna. She was a large, sturdy girl with light brown hair, bright blue eyes and a wide, easy smile. I couldn't remember ever telling her how to do her job and so she usually smiled at me as she cleared the plates. She seemed the wisest of the kitchen maids and had the air of one that knew things about men, itches and such.

The next morning, lurking near the kitchen, I saw her come back from the stable very early, with straw in her hair, her clothes in disarray and a smile on her face. She mentioned the name of one of the stable hands and giggled to the other girls about something I could not hear as she re-laced the bodice of her work dress. I longed to know exactly what she had been doing with him. She had a relaxed and satisfied look on her pretty face. I longed for that same look with every fiber of my being, or at least in a mysterious place where my two legs met.

I stayed behind to talk to Anna after supper that night, following her as she carried a stack of dishes to the kitchen.

"Anna," I said with my most squeaky of little mouse voices.

"Yes Miss?"

"I need some advice and I have chosen you to give it to me." My voice was stronger now, filled with false bravado.

Anna giggled. She put down the plates, wiped her hands on her muslin skirt, and dropped me a little curtsey. "Whatever can I help you with, Miss?"

"I think you have experience with men. I would like to know exactly what transpires between a man and a woman when...when...they are together, alone." I had somehow managed to get it out in one breath.

Her smile faded and a long look almost of contempt replaced it. "I don't know what you heard, but what I does on my own time is none of your affair."

"I meant no offense, Anna. I am sorry if I've suggested anything improper, but I have no one to ask about such things. You are the wisest of the kitchen girls."

I looked up at her humbly; I smiled. Flattery is a frightful weapon when used on one so unused to receiving it. The arrow hit its mark. Her blue eyes lost their flint.

"Of course, Miss, but a maiden such as yourself ought not to be interested in such base things. Someday you will marry a Nobleman and he will teach you what a wife ought to know. The doings of the lesser men and women ought not to concern you."

She turned to go. I reached out and grabbed a handful of her skirt. She turned, alarm and irritation on her face.. "Have you not seen the livestock mating? Surely you spend enough time at the stables to have seen something of what males and females do."

"Of course I have seen that, but that is not what people do... Is it?" The idea seemed impossible to me. It seemed more like fighting than loving. "That cannot be all there is," I begged. "That cannot be pleasurable."

"What do you know or need to know of pleasure?" she snapped.

"That is just it, Anna. I know nothing, and I must know. I cannot go on without knowing." My face flushed and tears welled.

"Oh no, miss. I will not be responsible for contributing to the ruin of any daughter of this Noble house. I bet you fancy you are in love with some lad or another, but ruin is all it will come to. Soon enough your parents will arrange your marriage, and all this will be for naught."

Anna took a step back, studied my face, and relented. "If you be needin' some plain facts, your father's library is full of books. Some from India and China have pictures and the like. I don't know much of readin', but I have dusted enough to be catching sight of the picture ones. On the top shelf next to the last window on the left, is a whole section of books on such things. I suppose it could not hurt for a girl to be prepared just a little." Anna smiled, and I knew I had chosen the right girl to confide in.

What an excellent suggestion, I thought. I had often sought answers in the vast walls of books. As I turned to go, Anna whispered, "Don't be tellin' who told you about them books. I don't need no trouble." I assured her I would not.

In the library, I found my father in the corner by the fireplace, deeply engrossed in a thick, red leather-bound volume so I crept back quietly into the hall to wait. He remained for just an hour, and I returned to find the books Anna had mentioned.. I spent the rest of that night and large parts of several others in my research, stealing candles from the kitchen for my nocturnal lessons.

Just as Anna promised, those shelves were full of wondrous books on anatomy, with explanations of different parts of both men and women. Thanking my Latin tutor for his diligence, I sat for hours in my father's goose-feather stuffed chair, devouring the pages. Not only the names but also the function of those bodily parts were revealed, illustrated with woodcuts and drawings.

My father's was indeed a very fine collection. The Text Anatomique explained much of the form with accurate drawings. I could verify the accuracy of female anatomy with my hand mirror, though I would have to wait to verify the descriptions of the male. It was not until I found the large leather tome from India that the drawings made complete sense. There were many pictures of males and females completely unclothed, partaking in various activities. Strangely enough, none of these served to scratch my itch. If anything, they fed my hunger.

One night, after hours of restlessness, I resolved to go to the stables the next day to see Antonio. I could think of nothing but page 728 in the Indian book and how I wanted to recreate that scene with him. I would lay beneath him with my legs spread wide like the picture and... I wasn't exactly sure what came next, but I had to find out. How he would look, feel, and taste were my only thoughts. The page's caption read "Gates of Heaven." I was sure such explorations would lead me closer to hell than heaven, but my faithful listeners, I cared not.

"I'd be glad to help ya scratch that itch," a man somewhere in the crowd yells out. A black glance from Bess. A piece of brown fruit sails through the air and strikes the heckler with a splat on the cheek. The crowd grows quiet again.

Leaving straight for the stables that morning, I planned to get Lillia to ride. It was a warm day, but unsettled and rainy. Alas, no soul could have stopped me from going. No rain would block my quest for the "Gates of Heaven."

By the time I reached the stables, the rain had begun to fall in torrents. My gown was soaked and muddy from the hem to almost my knees. It mattered not to me as I'd borrowed a plain gown and cloak from my mother's maid. Lillia was too old to ride in this rain so I chose another horse I knew to be a gentle mount. My usually blonde curls hung damp, limp and sparrow-brown with rain. My determination yielded not to weather or any force on this great earth.

CHAPTER SIX

As I approached the stables, I saw a knot of the stable boys just inside the largest stall leaning, slouching and laughing. Either they didn't recognize me in my drenched state and plain clothes, or they were in no mood to jump to attention at my presence. Most of the stock was inside the stable and work would be light on such a day. The boys fell silent at my approach. The short stout boy called Giavanni, looked at me and barked like one of father's hunting hounds. All the boys laughed.

"Antonio is busy right now," he said and resumed barking.

My heart sank. Where had he gone? No one else would do for my plan. The crowd of boys parted, and Antonio stood looking at me. Annoyance creased the raven's wings that were his brows and his usual smirk was nowhere to be seen. I walked straight up to him and said in my bravest voice, "I will go riding and I would have you accompany me."

At my announcement, all the other boys began to bark and howl. I Puzzled. I ignored them and tramped off through the mud to the stalls, with Antonio close behind. He took down a saddle and bridle and put them on the gentle mare I had chosen, looking at me all the while. His stare served only to quicken my heart and stiffen my resolve. I pulled my hood down to cover my face rather than have him see the excitement that must have shown on my face. He threw a blanket on a draft horse and led both horses out of the barn.

The rain was lighter now. I had carefully chosen the place of my education: a large grove of oak trees on the edge of the Estate. It took almost an hour to reach those trees through the rain and the mud. Pulling up, I tried to find some cover out of the rain for Rosy the mare. I wrapped her reins around the branch of a tall tree. She looked back at me with wide liquid eyes. She had never been out in the rain like this. A little white of fear shone around her eyes. She knew nothing of the true nature of the danger, or was she afraid for me? She snorted and threw her head as if in warning. Sliding off her back, I whispered in her ear and patted her flank. Antonio, already off the draft horse, had disappeared in to the thickest of the trees. This copse was completely untended. The trees were so thick that the fallen leaves covering the ground were dry in the deepest part beneath the oaks.

I slipped between two tree trunks and found him leaning against a thick tree trunk with his usual smirk adorning those full lips I longed to touch with mine. I had learned from my research that the activity I had come to learn usually began with kissing. He did not move, but stood waiting, watching me through dark lashes that shaded even darker eyes. My knees nearly buckled. My breath seemed to stop. No words were needed; none were spoken. Crossing the distance to him, my feet scarcely touched the ground. As I reached him, he opened his arms, enfolding me as I had dreamed night after night.

But unlike the Antonio of my dreams, this boy did not exclaim at my beauty or cover me with warm kisses as I had read about. Instead, he tore at my soaked clothes until I stood among the dark trees as naked as the day I came into the world, and with as little shame. Without a word, he brushed the tips of my breasts with his thumbs. Invisible cords seemed to lead from my breasts directly to the patch between my trembling legs. Each little brush of his thumbs caused a spasm in a secret place deep inside me. My lips parted and a small animal noise escaped. "Listen how the little bitch howls when in season," he said, his voice a husky whisper. Suddenly, the meaning of the stable boys' barking became clear. I would be embarrassed later. Just now I was approaching the "Gates of Heaven."

I knelt in the dry leaves and waited as Antonio knelt within inches of me. I could see even in the dim light no sign of a smirk. His eyes were nearly closed, and his breaths came deep and ragged. He loosed the fastening of his work britches and let them fall. The pictures in my father's books had not prepared me for what sprang forth. His phallus, as it was labeled in the books, was to those pictures as a candle is to the sun. It stood upright, begging me to touch it.

As I reached out to him, he grabbed my hand so tightly he nearly crushed my fingers. "I am in charge," he said. "I give the orders, my little spaniel bitch." Grabbing a handful of my wet hair, he pulled me to the ground. I yelped; then, whether with pain or passion, I began to sob.

Antonio's smirk reappeared. He spread my legs with his and moved in closer. I knew from the book what was about to transpire, but I was ill prepared for the reality. His hand brushed the little rosebud of flesh, whose name I could not remember. Waves of pleasure passed over me and I moaned. He laughed. The world disappeared; there was only Antonio's touch and my own cries. Suddenly, as I wished for the stroking never to stop, he thrust into me with one quick movement. Then he froze, as if with surprise, and said, "Never seen a virgin so hot. No matter. The deed is done and I will have my pleasure." From that moment on, I was a maid in name only.

His thrusts continued first short than longer until with a moan and a shudder, he collapsed on top of me. Was it over? I nearly screamed at him. He left me only hurt and wanting more. Antonio rose and moved away. "Who are you, little bitch?"

"I am Maria Gabrielle Constanzi, daughter to the Count and Countess of Pompeii." I had risen and was collecting what remained of my gown when I saw the stricken look on his face. His damp dark head was in his hands and he cried out loudly as if in pain. "Not again, please! God, tell me this is not so!"

"Who did you think I was? I have been to the stables often enough. You have seen me curry Lillia."

He raised his head from his hands as if to examine me closely.

"I should have looked more closely, but each time before, you appeared to be a haughty beauty. This time you are a..."

"Drowned sparrow in a muddy gown and ragged cloak?" I finished his sentence, and we both laughed until tears stained our cheeks.

That laughter broke the tension. Then Antonio sighed and spoke quietly. "It's always a woman. All my trouble and pain."

"You did not seem to me to be in pain."

"A moment's pleasure will most likely end in the loss of my position and at the very least a beating." he said, his beautiful eyes lowered.

"Why would you think that Antonio? I can keep a secret."

"It has happened before. Counts do not take kindly to the ruin of their daughters, even when they are truly bitches in heat."

"Is it so hard to control yourself?" I asked, as I sat on a fallen log sorting out my soaked clothes. He moved closer until I could feel the heat of him even as I shivered.

"Easier said than done when beautiful virgins drag me into the rain to deflower them in oak groves."

I flushed to think that a man as handsome as he would call me beautiful. Even now, in my pitiful situation, I cannot help but savor that precious memory. I fall quiet, but the crowd does not make a sound. Opening my eyes, I continue to speak, reprising that fateful conversation with my first love.

"Have you lost many positions?" I ask. I have drawn my cloak around me but I make no effort to don my clothes

"A few. I was born in the house of a popular courtesan in Venice. My father was a visiting Prince, my mother claimed, who now rules France as did the fourteen before him. It does not matter if I was a king's bastard. Children with no name have little value, no matter their sire. I was raised by an aunt and sent away from her house at the age of fourteen for some trouble with a nobleman's daughter. Do I have to paint a picture?" He raised his head and looked into my eyes with warmth that nearly singed me. I dared not answer.

"I have moved on many times and grow weary of it," he said. "I wish to live a simple life with just one woman someday, somewhere." But as he spoke, he moved closer. My eyes devoured his naked beauty.

"Is it so hard to have just one woman?" My voice was soft, and I did not meet his eyes.

"Women have a way of seeking me out, do they not? What am I to do when they drag me into the woods and lie naked at my feet? I am just a man, after all." The smile was back where it belonged on his handsome face, and he took my chin, raising my eyes to his.

"I will not tell anyone, Antonio. It is not my wish to see you hurt in any way."

"This cannot happen again. I will not be the cause of another noble daughter's ruin."

"Have there been so many?"

"Enough. It must not happen again." Yet he did not move away, and his eyes swept over me slowly.

"I have a way of getting what I want," I said daringly.

"And I am what you want? You are of noble birth." He seemed genuinely puzzled.

"It was my quest to scratch a strange itch and learn of men and women. You seemed the most pleasing teacher to me." We laughed again. The grove felt warmer to me now, and yet I shivered. Antonio put his strong, warm arm around my shoulders, pulling me close.

"Have you yet achieved your quest?"

"Not completely. I know more…and the itch has become a soreness, but it is still there." I watch his expression change.

This time was different. He took me gently in his arms, covered me with kisses and professed my beauty soft his voice against my ear. He seemed to care about my pleasure; every motion was slow and tender. He stopped occasionally to kiss my lips again and look deeply into my eyes. This time I saw not anger or need, only tenderness. When it seemed I could not stand the pleasure of another thrust, he quickened his pace. I felt the pleasure climax where our bodies joined. The most miraculous explosion, however, happened in my head. At last I understood. The itch was finally thoroughly scratched.

For a while, we lay entwined. Finally, Antonio spoke. "This cannot happen again." Then he kissed me deeply. "As you wish," I said, though I had no intention of keeping that promise. We dressed and rode back in silence.

That night I slept the sleep of the dead. Even now, on this scaffold, I can close my eyes, think of Antonio and feel a little twinge just where a lady never admits a twinge. If you think me without morals, it is because you have then never seen Antonio's eyes or felt those lips on yours.

Bess and several women near the front of the crowd cast visible sighs.

"The morning grows warm," I say. "I would be grateful for anything to rinse the dust from my throat. Gratitude, and the continuation of my story, are all I have to offer in return."

Spud reaches into his pack and produces a wooden cup. He runs to the well in the middle of the courtyard, fills the cup and scampers back to hand it up, with a look that says my smile is payment enough. I down the water in one gulp, then begin again.

CHAPTER SEVEN

The next day, I had planned to slip out early and go to the stables. The sun shone bright that morning and a ride seemed the best of all possible ideas. Surely I could change Antonio's mind about "never again." I stopped in the kitchen for some bread and a little cold meat to break my fast and discovered the entire staff of ten kitchen girls in various stages of mourning. Tears ran down their cheeks as they went about their chores, peeling, chopping, and stirring. I searched for the girl I trusted most and found Anna sitting on a stool, red-eyed and sobbing. "What's happened?" I asked.

"Antonio has taken his things and run off." She blew her nose on her sleeve.

"Some tart has broken his heart," said a tall, thin blonde girl. "He said he can no longer bear to stay." She laid down her knife on a mountain of peeled carrots and sniffed back tears.

"Well, maybe it was for the best," I said, with an air of maturity I could not have displayed even one day earlier.

"Oh Miss, you cannot know what we have lost," said Anna, crying on the stool beside the butter churn.

But I knew exactly the loss, and though I felt a little sad myself, I found I was grateful for the news. Indeed, it was hard not to smile as I cut a piece of bread and cold mutton and headed out of the kitchen's sunny warmth. Antonio, I felt, had left for my protection as well as his own, and I was grateful.

The itch, once scratched, did re-occur; but now I knew the secret. It was no longer a mystery of such import in my life. I looked forward with far greater complacency to the marriage my parents were arranging, and my days passed pleasantly with my music and my dreams.

The young nobleman my parents had chosen to be my husband came from Verona. Our family was much older and more respected, but his far richer. My mother explained that she did not wish to marry me to a much older man as she thought me to be a passionate soul. "Tomaso Terra is an exceedingly handsome young man, only thirty. He is well loved by all in his hometown. I am certain he will make you happy."

"As you wish, Mother," I said.

She cocked her head, a little puzzled at this change in me. She couldn't know how I longed to approach the "Gates of Heaven" again.

Preparing myself for the eventuality, I practiced my music, read and chose my trousseau.

Since the day of my birth, I had always been clothed in only the finest textiles, those being my family's business. Standing here in this plain muslin, I can but remember how fortunate I was once. Silks of every hue and numerous velvets were always available to me, and I took them for granted. It felt important before my marriage to choose my trousseau carefully. These would be the gowns of my new life. I loved the choosing, planning and fitting, and my days were filled with beautiful things. My happiness seemed perfect. It was during a particularly arduous fitting for a white velvet gown studded with pearls and amethysts I would wear on my wedding day that my ruin was discovered.

Sophia Bartolo was the best seamstress for many miles around, so of course she was engaged to make my gowns. She came to stay with us from Florence for as long as I had need. Each morning as I came into the room my mother had given

Sophia, I marveled at the new array of silks, satins and velvets spread about for me to choose.

We were weak acquainted; she had made gowns for me in the past for the most special occasions. As she carefully pinned the white velvet, she remarked to me, "Miss Gabriella has certainly grown in the bosom since last I sewed for her." I had not noticed. "And the miss is certainly much thicker at the waist." This change, too, had escaped me.

She stopped her pinning and looked into my eyes. "Oh well. Many a bride with a handsome fiancé goes to her marriage in such a condition."

My heart felt as if it had stopped. I had not even met my fiancé. There was no doubt; I'd known it the moment she spoke. I was with child. In complete and utter terror of that prospect, I ran to my room and wept.

I had known for years what causes pregnancy in animals. My recent visit to the oak grove with Antonio should have made me mindful of such a disastrous possibility, yet I'd been oblivious. My bleeding had never been at all regular. Now I realized with horror that the last time had been before Antonio left.

What was I to do? How could I present to a wealthy merchant's son the bastard child of a bastard stable hand? That the child's grandfather might be the king of France would, I suspected, make little difference.

It came to me, as I shed countless tears upon my bed, that I might try to hide my condition. My marriage was only two weeks away. I thought that this deceit was probably, as Sophia hinted, quite common in the whole of the world. This did not make such deception any less shameful, but never before had I been a deceitful person. The deceit, or perhaps the cause of it, resulted in my feeling ill and eating little. This change from my usual hearty appetite should have caused alarm within my family, but the preparations for the groom and his family's arrival eclipsed all other concerns. I lost enough weight to counteract the snugness of my new gowns, giving me hope that I could hide my condition for just long enough. I prayed to God each morning, on my knees in the chapel, for forgiveness and for my condition to stay a secret between my creator and me. Sophia was far too wise in the ways of the world to breathe a single word.

I watched from my window as the Terra family's caravan rode past, four wagons following behind. My heart raced at the thought of who sat inside that golden carriage.

Everyone and everything was ready for the glory of the presentation. The stone floors all over the house had been scrubbed until they gleamed. The blue and gold carpets in the reception room had all been freshly beaten. New tapestries were ordered and hung with grandeur, depicting glorious scenes of the Pompeii ancestors' many victories in battle. Enormous baskets of roses and lavender filled the corners of the room, providing delicious scents for this auspicious event.

My parents had politely allowed time for the Terras to collect themselves in the guest wing before the formal presentation. Presently we gathered in the reception hall, my family and principal servants, dressed in our finest in keeping with each person's station. My mother wore rich velvet the color of wine trimmed with ermine and pearls. My father stood tall and regal in his finest black velvet coat. Even my brothers looked like the little counts they would one day be, dressed in matching light blue velvet suits. I sought to outshine them all in a deep blue long napped velvet gown just matching the sky at evening fall. White rabbit, to symbolize purity, trimmed the neck of the gown. I could only hope it hid my lack of innocence. My heart pounded wildly, but no one would find my anxiety unnatural in these circumstances

When I saw Tomaso across the hall, I drew in a deep breath. I could feel my cheeks burn as he slowly walked across the room. He was not merely handsome, but glorious. Tomaso Terra was as beautifully made as Antonio and in much the same mold, but on a grander scale. Instead of black curls, he wore his dark mahogany hair in the new, longer fashion, reaching his shoulders in waves. He wore no wig, and I was glad of that, though it was the modern fashion. His chin was strong and his nose and brow regal. He looked at me with large, expressive eyes framed in dark lashes. In them I saw kindness and joy.

He took my mother's hand, kissed it and bowed deeply to my father. When he reached me, he dropped to his knees. I could tell the admiration in his eyes was not an affectation. He was well pleased with what he saw. I noticed his eyes lingered on my newly amplifed bosom. In my heart, the weight of my secret grew heavier. It would have been easier if he were not so handsome.

Then he reached for my hands and disaster struck. My dinner sought an immediate and violent exit from my stomach.

Clenching my teeth, I bolted for the kitchen, where I spent several long minutes on my knees, retching like a poisoned dog into the scrap bucket while the horrified kitchen staff looked on. When I finally stood, the white trim of my gown was fouled with vomit. I ran up the stairs with all the speed my retch weakened knees could muster.

When I returned to the great hall, I could not tell the state of things at first glance. My mother, ever the perfect hostess, appeared to have offered our guests some fabricated explanation of my inexcusable behavior. It seemed to have worked with Tomaso—I saw nothing but concern for my wellbeing in his beautiful dark eyes—but his parents were another matter. His father looked scornful, but it was his mother who would seal my fate.

She had the look of a shrewd woman, with the same dark eyes and mahogany hair as her son. Those eyes narrowed and swept over my figure like a hawk eying a rabbit. I drew myself up to my full height and smiled back at her. Whatever they thought, no one seemed disposed to dispute whatever story my mother had told them. The afternoon passed pleasantly enough and even supper was without incident. Tomaso was attentive and seemed not to believe his good fortune. He held my hand and looked into my eyes as we waited for the courses to be served.

"I cannot believe that God has blessed me with such a beautiful woman to be my wife. My mother tells me that you are a talented musician as well. My heart shall be yours alone, Gabriella, and I will spend each day of my life making you happy."

"I too feel blessed," I said, pushing my food around my plate.

"My family has a large home in Verona, and a new house in the country will be ready for you to choose all the furnishing to your liking in a few weeks."

"That sounds wonderful." Still, I dared not look up.

"Every night I will spend making you happy that you are my wife," he said softly, his mouth against my ear. "I have learned much of the ways of love and will enjoy teaching you everything I know."

At this, I could not help but look into his eyes. It was clear that he anticipated our wedding night, a scant week away. If I were not so ashamed and ill, I would surely have looked forward to that night, too. I hoped that Tomaso was not merely bragging and did indeed know many more ways to the "Gates of Heaven" than a stable boy.

I look out over the throng awaiting my execution. "Let this be a lesson to the more lustful and curious of you. Some things may indeed be worth waiting for.

Several of the crowd nod in agreement or impatience. None speak. They wait for my story to continue.

The next morning, I had not yet learned that lesson. I was happily making my toilet, arranging my hair in a fashion suited to one who would soon be a married lady, mistress of a great house. A knock came at my bedroom door. There stood my mother, and the look on her face changed my mood considerably.

"Gabriella, Tomaso's mother has brought their family physician. She has requested an examination to confirm your maidenhood."

Defenseless before her, I burst into the tears I'd been suppressing for days. When I finally stopped my sobs and met my mother's eyes, she no longer required an answer.

"Please forgive me, Mother. I never meant to soil the family name in this way."

My mother raised my chin with her soft hand and spoke quietly. "Oh my beautiful child, the name Pompeii has survived worse and will certainly go on. It is your life and happiness I care about." She reached over and took me in her arms. My tears fell like rain on her shoulder.

"Tomaso Terra would have been a good husband and your children would most assuredly have been beautiful. He would have provided well for you, and from the way he looks at you, he would have done much to keep you happy."

I dried my tears to answer the unspoken question in her eyes. "It was not even for love, Mother. I had an itch and longed to know what went on between men and women. It was but a brief experiment, but It has left me with child."

"Oh Gabriella." She closed her eyes and was silent for a long moment. Finally she looked up at me. "I bear some responsibility. Your father wanted to make this match a year ago and Tomaso's family was agreeable. It was I who wanted you to be a girl and have your music for a little longer. I should have known you were always in a hurry to know everything." She held me tighter against her. "The mysteries of love and life had too great a pull on you." She kissed my head. "I named you after an angel because you looked like one. I should not have expected you to act as one. A girl with such beauty and passion for life should have been better supervised." Her words though filled with love and concern, did little to soothe me.

"It would…not…have mattered… Mother. I could always slip away from any nurse or chaperon."

"That talent has cost you dearly, my girl. Dearly indeed."

After some time in my mother's arms, I pulled away and just listened as she had a right to lecture or even scold me. I deserved anything she chose to say and listened though my gaze was on the floor. "I was no maid when your father and I married. We were too much in love and lent seemed to go on forever that year. I had the luck of being barren for a time which became a curse once we married. You have inherited the fertility from your father's people, and your impatience from me."

Somehow this cheered me a little at the time. I was not a wanton; I was just fulfilling my destiny. I felt, for a moment, this disaster was not entirely my fault, and my heart lightened just a little.

CHAPTER EIGHT

The task of telling the Terra family there was to be no examination and thus no wedding fell to my mother, ever the family diplomat. Details were not discussed openly, but our house became a cold stone box with whispered disappointment and awkward silences in every corner. The Terra's family servants had just unpacked but began again to pack the wagons to leave. I watched the activity from the window of my chamber and shed many a tear.

My little brothers had been enjoying the novel activity, and I heard Richardo say to a small servant boy of the Terra's household. "Are you leaving because my sissy is a slut?" Though I knew he was repeating something he heard and couldn't really understand, and perhaps I deserved it, but the pain of those words spoken by his little boy lips cut deep. Younger brothers often tell you things you do not wish to hear. My tears so tenuously dammed, began to flow again. I would have rather he pissed in my eye as when he was a babe. These words hurt much more. Perhaps the pain was greater because I felt the truth of his words.

I watched as the wagons full of gifts departed, all three of them, but I didn't care about those things. It was the single mounted rider accompanying the coach who tore at my heart. Tomaso turned to look back at the house one last time with a stricken look that ripped my heart in two. For the first time, I fully realized that my reckless act had hurt an innocent man, one with whom I could have spent my life in happiness. It was inexcusable. Self-contempt, a new experience for me, would be the greatest punishment for my sin...or so I thought.

I did not leave my chamber for days. Spending a great deal of time on my knees, I confessed again and again, swore to change my shameless ways and begged forgiveness. After some days, I felt my prayers and tears had gone on long enough and left my future happiness in God's hands.

During my days as a recluse, I'd occasionally heard muffled voices outside my door. When finally I opened the door, I found that the boxes packed for my trip to Verona still filled my music room. Even more boxes had come to keep them company. It was only then that it dawned on me: plans had been made for me. All my instruments, books and music had been removed, and I assumed were contained in the packed boxes. It had never occurred to me that they would send me away. I had looked forward to a new life in Verona, but I'd expected to leave home with a husband. Was I now to leave alone?

I ran to find my mother.

Panicked, I rushed from room to room until I found my father in his library and demanded to know where mother was.

"She has left to see your aunt in Venice and make some arrangements."

"Arrangements for me?" I cried in disbelief.

"What do you think? You have ruined your future prospects. When this gets around—and make no mistake, it will—no noble son or gentleman of Florence will have you now as anything but his mistress." He got up from his chair without looking at me and walked to the window. "The life of a courtesan is not for a noble daughter of Pompeii. I will not have it!"

He turned toward me, his usual kind and thoughtful manner replaced with hardness and anger. I had never seen this side of him. The shock must have showed on my face.

"Why the look of surprise, Daughter? Did you think getting

yourself with child and causing pain and great shame to two families would not have consequences?"

I stood speechless.

"Some sort of life must be found for you," he said. His face was cold.

I dropped into a small chair beside my father's and stared at the floor, too hurt to speak. When I dared look up, my father's expression had softened. "Something must be done about whatever scoundrel did this deed. Do you love him so terribly? If so, I will see his punishment is light. He will be banished of course, unless it is your wish to be his wife?"

I lowered my eyes. "No Father, I did not love him."

"Did he force himself upon you? I will see him whipped within an inch of his worthless life and then hanged for such an evil deed!"

"No, Father."

His look of disappointment and pain cut deeper than the sharpest boning knife.

"Why then? Who was he?" My father's voice had gone quiet again. Somehow it was worse than the anger.

"I will not tell you his name. I will not see another hurt on my account. I had an itch, father, and I had to know." The blood pounded in my ears. My eyes bored into the floor and I prepared myself for any result. Any reaction from my father would have been justified.

My father threw back his head and laughed. He laughed as I had never heard before, with bitter irony in his tone, no mirth. When he finally stopped he said calmly. "It was Antonio, the stable hand. He ran off at about the right time. When I agreed to take him on, your aunt warned me he was bound to cause trouble. She sent him all the way from Venice to have him out of her household. I tried to tell your mother. She would not listen when I told her you were your mother's daughter."

My mouth fell open. I mustered all my courage and raised my eyes and my voice. "You will not say to me that any of this is mother's fault!"

He raised his hand and, although he had never hit me before,

I closed my eyes to receive the blow I deserved. No blow fell. My father's smooth, strong hand gently cupped the side of my face.

"I cannot blame you any more than I blame your mother. Your mother was once young, curious, and passionate, just as you are. She had the great luck to choose me rather than a stable boy for her adventures. We fell in love, and though promised to others the match was made. You were the most beautiful result of our love." I seemed to have a bottomless well of tears and more rolled down my cheeks. My father rose and made to dab them away with the hem of his silk shirt. "The problem is not so much what you have done; it is what others will think, and how you will be treated. An unmarried woman with no husband and a babe will be treated poorly. Those who were once your friends will be your friends no more. Men will assume you to be of loose morals. Your child will be called and treated as a bastard. In this world, our reputation is our life. I will not have such a life for you."

I spoke through sobs, "What...kind of...life...can I have?"

"You must leave here and go where no one knows you. Your mother is arranging a place at a convent school."

"I am to be a nun?"

"Well, we both know that would never do." He gave a little laugh. "No, you are to be a teacher. The Ospedale della Pieta is a fine music school as well as a convent. The students give performances and study with the best instructors. It may even be possible to meet a decent young man whom you could love and marry. It is in Venice. People in big cities are much more tolerant of scandal than we here in the country. With your beauty and your talent, a youthful mistake may someday be overlooked. Never here. In the country, people will judge you most unkindly. If your child is a girl, she can be raised at the school and learn music, too. If it is a male child, it can stay at the school until the age of sixteen and then be sent to learn a trade."

"Mother is arranging this?"

"Yes, she will be home in a few days."

"I suppose I deserve no say in this matter, Father."

"Of course you have a say. You may choose which day of next

week you will begin your new life." He took my chin and raised my eyes to his. "This babe is my first grandchild. I will not hear him called a bastard."

Though I knew full well that I was with child until this moment I had never thought of the child itself. It had been merely a word, but it would become a person long before I was ready. A new kind of fear clutched at my heart. Those of you with children know well this fear. I did not want to leave my home and all those I loved, but I had to leave. For the first time in my fifteen years, I thought of someone before myself. Even if my child was not yet in this world, I had to do what was best for him. I would go to this Ospedale della Pieta. I did not, however, need nor want anyone's pity.

In the next few days, awaiting my mother's return, I had far too much time on my hands. My music room was completely packed and riding had certainly lost its luster. The packing had been done for me and all that was left was to say my goodbyes and sleep. I found that I now required far more sleep than ever before. Who knew growing a child could be so tiring? I spent time with my brothers, who grew taller and more like little men each day. It made me sad that I would not be here to watch the rest of their journey to manhood. I would miss their running and playing in every room. I would even miss their unkind but honest words. One of the last things Ricardo said to me was, "I will miss you, Sissy, even if you are a slut." He said this while giving me his sunny and already devastating smile. Reassuring myself he really did not know what that word meant, I loved him anyway and kissed his sweet blond head.

CHAPTER NINE

When mother finally returned, she looked worn and uncharacteristically stern. Father met her at the door and after a quick embrace, they hurried off to their apartment to consult in private. Though not entirely slaves to rules, the count and countess never discussed important business in front of staff. I knew better than to interfere. When they were finished, they would send for me.

It took longer than I expected and when I was summoned to my father's library I found my mother with reddened eyes and her mouth set in a stern line. It did not bode well. Steeling my heart, I stood up straight. My duty was not only that of an obedient daughter to her parents. Now I must think as the mother of my child.

Tears come to my eyes. I look down at the three who had been my first audience, though there are now many rows of people come to watch. "I must beg your indulgence once. I can do nothing but continue my tale, but you have lives to live and matters to attend to. I am so grateful that you listen as I wait."

On Bess's face, there is rapt attention and perhaps even a trace of kindness. Marco, too, seems spellbound at my story. In the tiny man's eyes, there are tears. He reaches into his pack, and after some

digging, pulls out something white. He hands it up to me, a lace
handkerchief, white as snow and soft as eiderdown.

"Thank you, kindest sir. You cannot know how much I
appreciate your gift." I dab my eyes and Spud beams. The crowd
murmurs encouragement. I resume my tale.

All the arrangements for my travel were finalized and those at
the Ospedale della Pietà looked forward to my arrival, I was told.
The reason for my mother's tears was the most devastating news I
could imagine. Once I arrived at Ospedale, I could not come
home, and there would be no family visits. This news hit me like
the coldest winter wind. The Ospedale was a home for orphaned
girls who had no homes or families, and although I would be a
teacher, family visits were not allowed. I had lost my mother, my
father, and my brothers in one stroke.

My old life was forever gone. This was my true punishment. In
my heart, I felt the cold justice of the punishment. The fact that my
crime was not one of intention did not change the outcome. A price
must be paid for my actions. When I was told, I did not cry. I
accepted my father's words as if he had told me dinner would be late
and offered up a weak smile. This attempt caused my mother to
crumble into my father's arms, tears staining the dark velvet of his
waistcoat. Again, I drew myself up. If I could not be strong, I could
at least pretend to be. That pretense would become a new weapon in
my arsenal. One must gather weapons to fight the war that is this life.

All my things were packed and though I did not want to
leave, I reasoned that the sooner I left my former life, the sooner
my new one could begin. A pretense of good spirits was the last
gift I could give those whom I had caused so much pain. My false
cheer served me, too. Pretending all was well, I began to feel
better. I did my best to smile at the parting and held no one but
my father's embrace for more than the briefest moment.

I knew it was important that my journey began before the
weather grew colder and I grew larger. My experience with travel
was limited to the few hours ride it took to reach Florence. The
journey to Venice would take days.

Our family's most comfortable and lavish carriage was prepared for me and I was allowed to take one lady's maid on my journey. Although she could not stay with me, it comforted me to have Angelina. She was Mother's favorite and I knew Mother would miss her dearly. She was kind and, though not much older than I, knew much of the world. Without her soft grey eyes looking into mine and her hand to hold, the long journey would have been near unbearable.

Three wagons of belongings followed behind. My pianoforte took up one entire wagon but could not be left behind. It was the one passion I had left to me.

The first day of travel was pleasant. The weather was warm for winter, the buds on the trees swelling with each warm day. My father sent his two best coachman and three wagon drivers with me. One of the drivers seemed especially attentive and always hurried to help me up or down the wooden carriage step. He was younger than the others and I was grateful for his help and attention until I chanced to meet his glance. Though the best of the lot, his clothes were dirty and ragged, and by the smell of him, he could not have bathed in weeks. He leered at me, behavior wholly inappropriate to my previous station. Though I did not entirely grasp this new truth, his look made my skin crawl.

The road was good, and I gazed out the window at the passing countryside that I might never see again. When I managed to close my eyes, I saw my mother's grief-stricken face, felt my father's arms, and watched my little brothers wave goodbye one last time. A second day on the road to Venice brought more of the same. I accepted the rhythm of the road and wondered about my future life and what lay ahead.

This road was not commonly travelled this time of year and I grew tired of counting crows in the naked tree branches. As I dozed and the carriage bumped along, a remarkable and wondrous thing happened. Something fluttered in my rounding belly and woke me from my drowsing with a start. Angelina found my reaction comical and explained once she stopped laughing. "At a certain time, a babe will make itself known by moving. This is a good and natural thing." I was surprised and somehow pleased. In my homesickness and misery, I had not thought of the babe in some time, and I felt happy to put my hands on my belly and feel this movement.

Once it made its presence known to me, the babe did not want to be forgotten again and seemed in constant motion. Even when I slept, he moved. I began to think of the babe as a boy. I wished for a child that would look like one of my parents or even my brothers: a constant reminder of home that I would have with me.

As we traveled north and east toward Venice, the air grew colder. The snow gathered on the majestic mountains visible in the distance to the north. We stopped often, but one night the weather forced us to set up a camp rather than head on to pass the night in some comfortable inn as we had always done before. In such primitive surroundings, one makes do with few personal comforts. I was making do by squatting behind some tall weeds when suddenly hands grabbed me from behind. Someone threw me to the ground and I found myself on my back with my skirt and petticoats around my waist. The attentive wagon driver stood over me. I recognized the nasty expression on his dirty face.

"Quiet Girl! It's just a bit of fun and no one the wiser."

For a moment I was stunned by his display of impudence. How dare he talk to me in such a tone, let alone drop to his knees and begin to unfasten his britches? In the time it took for him to draw one breath, I had pulled out the little gold handled knife my father had given me at our parting and pressed it to his throat. I was fast, my childhood training in arms not entirely forgotten.

"Be gone! Or this blade will insure this is the last bit of fun you ever have." As he made to rise, I sliced his neck a little to help him remember not to try to steal "a bit of fun" from some other poor girl. He yelped and scurried backward off into the darkness with his pants still down around his ankles.

As I arranged my garments, I realized my whole body shook with shock. The little dagger in my hand gleamed by the cold light of the winter's moon. "Always keep it near for protection," my father had whispered, as he pressed it into my hand. Now I understood why. No impudent wagon driver would have dared speak to me, let alone touch me, when I was the chaste maiden daughter of a count. My father's quiet strength and capable manner had always been the rock upon which I moored the leaky little boat of my previous young life. Now my father was not here to protect me; I had to protect myself, and I could. I was not only my mother's passionate daughter, but my father's strong one as well.

The next morning, the wagons moved on, one driver short. Niko, the old coachman, did not take kindly to driving a wagon but did what had to be done. With the colder air came freezing winds. We stayed a day longer at a humble inn the next night to make sure there would be no camping in the cold, to my great relief. It was only one more day until we reached Venice, Niko told me as he helped me down, with his eyes respectfully downcast.

I felt great excitement well within my heart. I had never been to Venice and was looking forward to all such a large and exotic city had to show me. I had been to Florence so often that, though fairly large, it held no mystery for me. I did not know what was to come, but I was far more excited than afraid. Baby Antonio, as I sometimes called the child with in me, seemed excited too, as his constant motion sped up. It wasn't painful. I felt comforted by the notion that I was not alone in my adventure. This babe was part of me, and I loved him. He would certainly be beautiful. Counting back the weeks, I realized I had just a few months to wait until I held him in my arms.

One more inn, one more day of jolting down the high road. As we grew nearer to Venice, the roads grew wider and much smoother, and I was grateful. As we passed the outskirts of Verona, I felt a deep pang of regret for all I had lost. As I examined the lines of grand stone houses, I wondered which one was Tomaso's as the rivers of carriages flowed by as I mourned the happy and comfortable life that would never be mine.

We came to the end of the land and our little caravan pulled up. There, obscured slightly by a layer of mist on the lagoon, stood Venice, surrounded by water. We transferred to boats to get to the Oespedale. Angelina and I got into a small, two oared gondola painted bright red. The wagon's contents would be loaded into larger boats and follow later. The only way to Venice was by boat, I knew, but I could not take my eyes from the wonder of the sight as our boat drew near and the mist cleared. There upon the turbulent winter sea sat the Most Serene Republic, as Venice was called. The buildings came up to the water's edge with no visible space between. In front of each building was a dock for boats. Boats surrounded the city like bees around a hive; large ones, small ones, buzzing everywhere.

The majority of the buildings were large, three stories at least. In the distance, domes and towers of great churches pierced the surface of a sea of red tiled roofs. All were built of stone, but unlike my family's plain gray stone house, most were painted colors. Pink, yellow, beige and rust, these lovely colored structures reminded me of all the pretty gowns of my trousseau. Each house or shop adorned with intricately carved arches that hung like the lace and ribbon trimmings. I stared with wonder as the sun reflected off the red roofs. It seemed a fairy land, not quite real. It was only as we drew close enough to see the residents of this magic place that I knew it was not a dream.

Ordinary people went about their business. Some swept the streets, if that is what one calls the space between buildings. Others carried goods in baskets or rolled carts. What wonders could be found along the narrow streets carved out between those painted stone confections? It would be heaven to walk among those lovely arches and see where the little paths and bridges led, but I doubted convents allowed such exploration.

We were rowed past the ornate buildings and stopped at a rather plain four-story structure built of gray stones. The Ospedale della Pieta Convent was a cluster of one large and several smaller buildings, arranged in a rectangle and bordered on one side by a low stone seawall. Where the seawall stopped, there was a higher wall, and a tower looked over the rest of the complex. The main building was of stones with no arches or adornments. The tower gave the whole of the place a stark look of a military encampment I saw once in a book. The windows on the side facing the sea were small and simple. The place looked cold and austere. My heart sank. How, in this lovely fairytale city, was I to live in this fort of gray stone?

As the boat pulled nearer, I heard music from several directions at once. From the left came the sounds of strings played both in harmony and as solos. The sounds from the right were of a large chorus singing something I had heard before but could not place. I had arrived at my new home to be greeted with music from every direction. What mattered a plain building if a musical paradise were housed within?

The boat pulled up to the dock and a small party approached. A little black-haired girl, no more than six, ran to meet us, waving and shouting and standing on tip toes. She shouted as the boat approached, "Are you the new teacher, Miss? The old one died three months ago and we are falling behind in our lessons. We have The maestro for the violin, but we need a keyboard teacher. The hautboy is boring and I do not like the recorder much. Will you teach the harpsichord?" The little girl finished her rapid series of questions as I disembarked. She did not bother to wait for answers but grabbed my hand and pulled me up the large stone steps from the dock. I turned to bid good-bye to Angelina, but the boat was already bearing her away across the water. Perhaps it was for the best. I had learned how much good-byes hurt.

"You're very fat. Are you going to have a babe? I like babies," the little girl said as we climbed the steps. "We have none at the Ospedale, not anymore."

At the top of the steps stood a short, stout woman in a habit of rough gray wool. She smiled with her arms spread wide. "Welcome to the Ospedale della Pieta. I am the Head Mistress Sister Angelica. We welcome our new teacher. Come, my dear, you must be tired from your journey. One of your eager students will show you to your room."

I was exhausted and while I yearned to see everything, rest had to come first. My child demanded it. On the way to my room, I noticed that my first impression had been mistaken. The

Ospedale looked more like a little town than a soldier's camp. There were pens for animals, stone cutters sheds, a large blacksmith and forge, all that was needed to make the place self-sufficient. There were even small patches of dirt that must have grown vegetables in the warmer season. The single-story buildings I guessed must be dormitories. The four-storied main building must be the music school, judging by the lovely music pouring out of open windows. There was a rectory, the little girl told me, where all males of the town must be housed.

The convent was even plainer than the rest of the structures, I noticed as we walked by. "The sisters all live there," my child guide said. "I don't think I want to be a nun. Gray wool is just too itchy. There is an infirmary there, too, where the sisters care for the sick. Once, I stayed there for three days when I ate bad pork. My name is Maria Rosa."

At last we arrived at our destination, a room in one of the single storied buildings. It was barely furnished, but on a small table beside the bed, someone had set tea, bread, and hard cheese. I doubted my belongings would fit in this modest chamber. Certainly there was no place to hang the tapestry of my Grandfather's great victory against invaders in the hills of Mantua. I bolted down the simple meal and collapsed on the little narrow bed. The pillows were woven of some rough fabric, nothing like my silk linens at home; but this did not delay my sleep for more than a few seconds.

Awakened the next morning by someone knocking at the door, I hurried to answer. In the hall stood the most beautiful girl I had ever seen. She was not much taller than Maria Rosa and her blue-black hair hung in soft waves to her waist. She wore a plain muslin jacket and laced vest over matching bloomers. The small, heart-shaped face that greeted me was pleasing, but it was her eyes that were extraordinary. They were the deepest blue I could ever imagine. She gave me a smile that did not quite reach those exquisite eyes. There was an odd coldness in them.

"I am Veronica." She reached out and clasped my hand warmly with both of hers. Perhaps I had imagined the chill. "We will be the best of friends. My room is next door and we are the same age. Most here are younger or much older. I have brought you tea and some bread and meat to break your fast. You must drink all your tea to ward off the chill, which is very bad here in winter." The girl reached into her pocket and produced three lumps of sugar. "I managed to nick some sugar from the kitchen, if you would like."

"Yes, thank you." I held the cup out to her and she dropped in the lumps.

"I begged us out of morning prayers. I said you were still too tired and required my help to unpack. You don't mind my little lie, do you?" She glanced at me coyly through raven lashes, and I knew she was right. We would be friends.

After I finished my food and all the strong, bitter tea, Veronica took me on a tour and explained how things were at the Ospedale. "There are two parts to the school. One is for the common girls, who live in a large dormitory and study basic things like cooking and sewing. This one is for girls of noble blood. We are treated to the finest musical education." We had arrived at the tall building from which music seemed to come from everywhere at once.

"Does noble blood matter here? Are not all orphans?" I asked as we climbed to stone stairs to the top floor.

"Noble blood always matters. Did you not arrive with three wagons full of treasures? Surely these are not the belongings of a peasant girl." Veronica gave me a look of certainty. "Your noble blood is why you have your own quarters and will teach, as do I. No drafty shared common dormitory for us."

She stopped talking and looked at me as if taking the measure of my every feature. "Don't we make a pair? You are as fair as I am dark. You are as tall as I am petite. Your green eyes make a beautiful contrast to mine of sapphire. We would certainly add many admirers to the usual concert attendees."

Veronica stopped at a room with half a dozen harpsichords. In front of each, sat a little girl on a bench. The musicians could not have been much older than six or seven. Some of the girls sat swinging their feet that did not nearly touch the floor. All their tiny fingers flew over the keys with varying degrees of enthusiasm. The sounds they produced were far from accomplished, but it made me smile to think I might teach them.

"I heard you brought a pianoforte," said Veronica. "It will be the first for our school. I have never even seen one." Veronica stood by patiently as I went from classroom to classroom, peeking in to observe girls of different ages learning and practicing. Veronica tugged on my sleeve, and I turned toward my guide and new friend. "What do you play beside the pianoforte?" she asked. "The violin, of course, but what else?"

I flushed at the mention of the violin. That was the least of my talents, for now I kept that to myself. "I love the recorder; I am passable at the hautboy and I am told my voice is pleasant. My best instrument is the harpsichord. I am still learning the pianoforte myself."

"Well, we dearly need a keyboard teacher. As you can see, these little urchins are all but torturing those poor instruments. Our old teacher dropped dead at the keyboard, so it is certain you will teach. What position you play at concerts will be determined by your audition."

"Audition?" I inquired.

"Oh yes. Just because you brought us a pianoforte and will teach students to use it, does not mean you will perform. There are many here with great talent," Her dark blue eyes bored into me.

"What do you play, Veronica?"

"I play only the violin. My talent would be wasted on anything but the most beautiful of instruments. The maestro agrees. It is the maestro who will conduct your audition, as he does all the auditions." She had an air of confidence that bordered on arrogance. Confidence in one's talent is not a bad thing, I thought, but I would hear her play before I accepted hers as warranted.

My new friend gave me a cursory tour of the rest of the

Ospedale, and I was pleased to see what a busy and productive place my new home was.

Heading back toward the room I had been assigned, I began to feel strange. My head spun. I realized with a start that I had not felt little Antonio move at all since last night. As I put my hand on my stomach, a sudden pain doubled me over. Something warm ran down my legs and at my feet I saw a growing puddle of bright crimson. The world went black.

CHAPTER TEN

I stop speaking. Remembering the pain and the loss is almost too much for me to bear, but my eyes are dry, having no tears left to cry. The crowd is silent. The blacksmith takes a small bottle from his pocket. He approaches the stage to hand it up to me. It is a dark bottle with a cork. I pour some of the contents into the empty wooden cup and take a sip. It is a strong sweet wine. I drink deep. As I look down at the young man's face, he nods as if to say, "For courage." I continue.

"I awoke in a room I did not remember, surrounded by strangers with expressions serious as the grave. I remember the pain; I remember thinking it could not be the babe, as it was much too early for him to be born. A woman in gray held my hand. "Your child is coming. You must be strong now," she said. After another blinding pain, something seemed to rip inside me and the world went dark again. In pain and darkness, I heard a voice say: "It is too soon. He cannot live." The last sound I remember was a woman screaming with the most terrible grief. I know now the screaming came from my own lips.

Later, days or weeks later, I opened my eyes. This small action took far too much effort, and I simply closed them again. How many times this happened and over what period of time I do not know. Eventually, I became aware that I was alive and my rounded belly was now flat. I also knew that while I lived, my babe did not. At that moment, a hole in my heart opened that would never entirely heal. My child was gone. I knew that whatever became of the rest of my life, that pain would always be with me. I closed my eyes again.

When I open them again this day, I see that the assembled faces are grave. A tear glistens on Bess's ruddy cheek. I sit in silence, unsure if I can continue. Then Spud approaches, holding in his small dirty hand a little ivory recorder, the sort a child might learn to play on. I take the recorder from his hand and try a few notes.

It is a lovely, well-made little treasure with carvings of vines running the length of it. Its tone is bright. I remember a sweet tune I once learned on a little instrument much like this and I play it. Then another tune, more complicated than the first, but I pare the composition down to its barest melody line. I play with every breath I have, my eyes closed, bathing in the lovely notes that fill the warm summer air. Though it is not much of a performance, my heart soars. I have played very little since the tragic day…But I will not get ahead of myself.

The playing heals my heart just enough as playing music always does. I look down at the little man who had somehow known exactly what would soothe me best. He smiles up at me, gives a little nod. When I hand him back the instrument, he begins to play. Fingers flying, he fills the air with intricate notes, playing the same little tune as I, but with each note of the work, fully and joyfully represented.

I smile down at Spud, another soul who knows the true-life sustaining power of music. I grow brave enough to continue.

I must have been unconscious for a long while after my ordeal. Gradually I became aware sometime later that I was not alone in my chamber. I sat up, and a thin woman in a gray woolen habit rose from her chair at the foot of my bed. She put down her rosary and rushed to my side. "Oh miss, we did not think you would return to this world. I have never seen anyone lose so much of their life's blood and live. You must be of strong stock."

"My child is dead?" I asked, knowing full well the answer. The pain I felt in my heart would not have been there if he lived.

"Yes, my child, it was far too soon for him to live. It was a boy, and we buried him in the Garden of Innocents. When you are stronger I will show you where. It is my special mission to pray for expectant mothers and babes when they are lost."

Even though I knew this to be true, the words made fresh my pain. I said nothing. For several days I went mechanically about the business of recovery: eating, bathing, even walking a little without saying a word. My heart was empty.

One day, Veronica came to visit me just after I had ventured down the hall for the tenth time that day in an attempt to gain strength. "I am glad to see you look rather well, Gabriella. I have missed you, and the girls are anxious to start their lessons." I looked at her beautiful, smiling face without replying.

"Come now," she said, "do you think you are the only woman ever to lose a babe? I have seen it many times. You need to be grateful that you still breathe." Her casual dismissal of my loss hurt me. But she came to my side and took my hand. "We miss you and need you."

I began to cry. The tears seemed to wash away some of my sadness. The hole in my heart would always be there, but now a new life called.

I dried my eyes. "I have missed you, too. How long has it been since..."

You have been here for three weeks, although we were not sure you were going to live through the ordeal. I am so glad you will recover."

"I am no weakling. I must make the best life possible for myself," I said, hoping my words would make it come true.

"That's the spirit. No one who survived as you have, could be anything but strong." Veronica hugged me tight. She'd been raised without parents, I thought. How could she know the right thing to say? I forgave her for her coldness and her wounding comments.

Each little step I took gave me more strength. Each day, I felt a little more like myself. The pain in my heart was not the focus of my being, though it never left. I pushed it down inside me, pulling it out sometimes when I was alone.

While I was unaware, a great deal of activity must have taken place around me. My belongings were placed in my new room. This room held my things perfectly. My furniture from home was here, and even my soft silk and satin pillows were where they belonged. The tapestries from home had been hung on the walls, though not where I would have chosen. No matter. I would instruct someone later where they should be. I found that the clothes from my trousseau were unpacked and placed in my wardrobe. Beside them hung some new and plainer things more appropriate for life at the Ospedale. My hautboy, recorder, violin, and even my harpsichord had been placed in the parlor next door I shared with Veronica. The pianoforte must have been moved to the practice room where it belonged for all to play.

The routine of the school consumed me and my new friend, Veronica, was by my side. She came into my room each morning before prayers to tell me the gossip of our little town. I shared with her stories of my home and family. When we managed to arrive on time, the days started with morning prayers, breakfast, then lessons. Teaching the youngest girls the harpsichord, cheered me. I loved to see them learn the notes, and I delighted in their progress. I would make them the best musicians possible. Their little fingers stretching as far as they could made me smile almost every day. My pianoforte students were older girls, for students were not allowed to progress to the piano until they had mastered other instruments. Unskilled fingers would not be allowed to accost our school's most precious new acquisition. My youngest pianoforte pupil was ten, and many were older than I.

After lunch came more lessons and chores until evening vespers and supper. The nuns that cooked for the Ospedale were talented indeed, and it did not take me long to fill out my clothes again.

All the girls and women, from six to sixty, wore the same

clothes: a white cotton ruffled blouse, knee-length skirts with ankle-length muslin bloomers. Only the sisters wore gray habits.

In the evening, the performances took place. The choir and orchestra were excellent and students performed each evening, pieces they had prepared that day. This normally happened in the chapel. It was a large room with many tall windows of deeply colored glass. Angels looked down on me from those windows and from paintings on the walls. I felt no scorn from those angelic observers. I had paid the price for my sin.

There was a large, beautiful concert hall reserved for special occasions. An attentive audience made up of curious music lovers and wealthy patrons filled the chapel on these special occasions. At our nightly concerts, the patrons sat behind wooden screens, as in any convent. We could not see them, but we all knew they were there. It was on one of these evenings I heard Veronica play the violin.

Veronica's performance was a revelation. She moved her bow arm with the speed and precision I had never witnessed. The beautiful girl and the instrument were one, and the effect was magnificent. She performed a piece I had attempted myself many times, a sonata by Antonio Vivaldi. I had suspected its beauty when I had read the notes in my music room at home, but never dreamed how beautiful it could be in Veronica's hands. Tears came to my eyes. I would never question her talent again. What I'd thought was arrogance was simply an expression of the truth.

I would never again consider myself Veronica's equal. In all things musical, she was my superior. I was content to accompany the singers on my harpsichord and drink in the other performances.

Though we were the same age, she seemed much wiser in the ways of the world than I. Considering I was raised on a country estate, she took it on herself to teach me what I needed to learn of the world. When our days' duties ended, Veronica and I would go to my room and talk over the day, staying up far past our appointed time. She showed me how to cover my window with blankets so the candle we burned could not be seen, and we would talk and giggle until one of us fell asleep. She usually fell asleep in my bed and left sometime in the night. I found it a little strange that I was never invited to her room, but after all, mine was larger, and I doubted her orphan's bed had silk pillows.

She told me she was the daughter of a prized courtesan and a royal patron. Born in Verona in secret, she came to the Ospedale at the age of six after the death of her mother. She said no more of her mother and I, assuming the subject was painful, did not ask. Veronica had played the violin and only the violin from beginning. The maestro, sometimes called "The Red Priest" because of his red hair, was her first and only teacher. "He writes for me alone," Veronica said, a smug look on her face. "He composes for all the other instruments and our Orchestra, but his violin works are for my hands alone." This surprised me, but I did not doubt Veronica's word.

I told her of my home and of the itch and Antonio. She held my hand when I could not help but cry... when the pain became too great. I had never known such friendship.

CHAPTER ELEVEN

One evening after dinner, my friend said to me as we snuggled beneath my soft covers to share our gossip, "It is time you had your audition, I have spoken to the maestro of your beauty and he is anxious to see you perform."

"What is the beauty of a woman to him?" I asked. "Is he not a priest?

"The Red Priest is still very much a man," she answered.

As I made the long walk to the rectory carrying my recorder and violin, my hands shook. I would have to use the other instruments provided, I could not carry my harpsichord and the heavy hautboy. Taking a deep breath, I reminded myself who I was. Maria Gabriella Constanzi Pompeii would audition for this maestro with pride. I held my head high and said a little prayer as I knocked upon the door.

He opened the door and greeted me with a warm smile. He appeared much younger than at our performances, where he wore an ornate white wig as was the fashion. His auburn hair was neatly trimmed, and he seemed much taller from up close, with the wide-shouldered, muscular physique of a workman rather than of a priest. But he was a priest, I reminded myself, however handsome.

I headed to the music stand. My own harpsichord and hautboy had been set up for me, an unexpected kindness.

He crossed the room and stopped behind me, placing his hand on my shoulder. My cheeks burned. "Gabriella, I am so glad to finally hear you play. On the music stand is a piece I wrote for your audition." I ran over the notes, hearing them in my head. They were so familiar and so dear to me, and still I was shocked to read the signature below the score. This page was signed Antonio Vivaldi.

I played the harpsichord as if in a dream. I played the keyboard deftly. When I had finished, he did not speak a single word, but handed me another piece, this one for the violin. It seemed not overly difficult, and I made my best attempt, but if you have been paying attention to my tale, you can guess how that sounded. Next, he handed me music for the hautboy and for the recorder. Finally, I was asked to sing a short piece of my choosing.

When all was finished, I sat in judgment before Father Vivaldi, as I now knew him to be. This was the man who had written some of the greatest music I had ever known, the man of whose music I often dreamed. How I dreaded his assessment.

He began with a sigh, a kind smile, and a glint of amusement in his brown eyes. "Well, my lovely child, you do have talent. Your voice is pleasant, and your recorder and hautboy are quite adequate. It is in your keyboard, that your greatest virtues emerge. The passion with which you play the harpsichord would certainly be even more suited to the pianoforte. As for your violin, I suggest you donate it to the less fortunate. It would be a disservice to that fine instrument to torture it further."

At the look on my face, the maestro threw back his head and laughed the hearty laugh I cannot forget even upon this gallows. After a moment, I found myself laughing with him, for I knew he spoke true.

"The violin is certainly not my best instrument," I admitted. "I know the notes, but no matter how I try, I cannot make them sound sweet. I hear the fault, but the notes are already in the air, never to be taken back. Practice does not seem to help."

He reached over, picked up my violin and played the simple little piece with true mastery. As I watched him play, I realized I had seen that look of complete absorption and unequaled passion on the face of another Antonio, and during a very different activity. My first Antonio had destroyed my future. This one, the handsome musical genius, was a priest. This attraction I felt for him was a danger to my mortal soul.

Our session came to an end all too quickly, but with the assurance that others would follow. I hurried back to my chamber to find Veronica waiting, anxious to hear about my audition. I told her all that happened.

She considered carefully. "None of that was unexpected. You really are quite good at the keyboard. Did he take your violin from you and break it?"

"No. But he encouraged me not to continue to torture it further." We both laughed.

"No one can compare to your pianoforte, and I am sure he will write new works for it," said Veronica.

I told her of my joy at finding the Red Priest was my own favorite composer. I did not mention my unholy attraction to his handsome person. This was a thought for me alone and perhaps the Lord Satan. Veronica shared my delight at Maestro Vivaldi's opinion of my talent and we headed off to our respective duties.

Most of my lessons took place in the morning, and now that I was stronger, I had chores assigned to me. Never participating in the daily work of the estate in the past, I knew little of such activities. It was during a trip to the garden to fetch some fresh vegetables I realized a miracle had occurred. I was humming and my heart felt light again. This had not been so since I first discovered my condition long months ago.

I enjoyed doing simple things to help my new community. I possessed few skills at the daily tasks and so was relegated to simple errands. Unfortunately, my laundry audition was as bleak as my violin playing.

"Do you think the sheets clean themselves?" said Marta, the head washer woman one morning as I stopped by to deliver sheets to the laundry. She stood stirring the huge steaming pot full of something foul smelling. The gathered girls laughed as I wondered at the huge vats of steaming water and sheets. "This be how we cleans them, your royal highness." Marta leaned the thick branch she used for stirring against the kettle and wiped sweat off her brow. Her iron-gray hair hung damp and limp below the kerchief she pulled back a bit to keep her hair out of her eyes. She stood smiling, as if she could not wait to hear what I had to say.

"What is that terrible smell?" I said, dropping the bundles I carried into a huge pile and pinching my nostrils tight between my finger and thumb.

One of the girls pointed to a bucket, undeniably the source of the odor.

"It's lye soap." Marta stopped her stirring. "Made from sheep fat. It takes strong stuff to get out the stains you fine ladies gets on your sheets."

"Have you never seen laundry done?" said little Maria Rosa, whose job it was to ladle the stinking gray lye soap into the enormous kettle. The other three girls laughed at that prospect.

"How could she?" Veronica said. She had brought another bundle to be washed and now stood beside me. "She was born a countess on a fine estate, not left at the gate in a basket like you three."

"Pardon me, countess." All three of the girls bowed low, laughing until they had not breath to continue.

Although I knew little of laundry, cooking and such things, I could not resist giving advice; such is my nature. "Could not something be found to clean the sheets that doesn't smell so bad? Perhaps if you left them to bleach in the sun, they would certainly be clean and fresh smelling."

Marta picked up the stick and began to stir once again. "Why did I never think of that? Do you think if the sun could clean sheets, I'd stand here stirring this stink 'til my eyes burn red? Off with you, girl, we have work to do."

Because of my ignorance and natural bossiness, the girls continued calling me 'Countess'." Never having had a sister, I did not mind the teasing, really. I relished being part of the sisterhood of the Ospedale della Pieta, with the help of Veronica to defend me.

As I fetched various items, carrying things here and there, I reveled in the freedom. I loved talking with the many workers it required to keep our little beehive buzzing. The girls that tended the chickens told me which hens were laying and why. Those hanging laundry would wave but never ask for my help. When I took the eggs to the kitchen, the cooks would sometimes give me a small slice of fresh bread with honey. I thought my job the best of all.

Some of the workers were male, and not all were old. I had given little thought to my previous itch since I came to the Ospedale. I did not miss the feeling that had brought me so much trouble: desire, Veronica called it. As I hurried past the blacksmith's barn from the chicken coup, something caught my eye. It was a man stripped to the waist, working by the roaring furnace. He swung a large hammer to flatten an iron implement that glowed red at the end. I stopped so suddenly I dropped my basket. He turned, stared, then smiled. "You must be the 'Countess'." He doused the glowing red implement in water and picked up a rag to dry the sweat from his chest and hands. I inhaled the scent of him as he came near.

He reached over to pluck a chicken feather from my hair and looked amused. "Tell me, does my smithy fascinate you?"

"I am always interested in learning, and there is much of interest in this smithy." I reached down to rub a scratch on my arm inflicted by the largest and meanest of the hens.

The blacksmith took another step toward me, and it struck me how he must have understood my words. He reached down and gently lifted my arm to examine the scratch.

"You are hurt." His voice held tenderness.

"It is nothing. Some of the hens do not relish me stealing their babies. It is just a scratch." He was very close to me now. I saw the danger; it can't be said that I didn't see it. His light brown hair was curly and seemed to surround his head like the rays of the sun, wild and handsome. His wide shoulders were corded with the muscles of hard work. These shoulders tapered to a lean waist by way of a similarly muscled chest. You are right to think such a sight had caused me so much trouble once before and that I should have walked on quickly. This gallows where my life will end attests to my inability to avoid trouble, so please indulge me as I remember. His britches were wet from his effort and the heat of the furnace, and so hid little of his masculine attributes. It was his dark blue eyes and warm and generous smile, which I remember even now that woke the old hunger of desire that caused my previous doom.

I tore my eyes away from him and said, "I must get these eggs to the kitchen."

"You may grace our humble smithy with your noble presence any time, countess." The sound of his laughter followed me nearly to the kitchen.

I questioned Nina, my favorite of the cooks. She seemed to know much that she was eager to share.

"His name is Raphael. Ain't he a handsome thing? He's not really a smithy at all. He's the Overseer of all the equipment that isn't musical." She picked up one of my eggs and cracked it into a large brown bowl. "He must have been repairing something he did not trust the apprentices to attend. Raphael can do nearly anything that needs doing around here, but mostly he has more important things to do. I certainly wouldn't mind him repairing me a little." She cut a piece of warm bread, drizzled honey onto it and handed it to me. I decided it wise to steer clear of the Ospedale's handsome overseer. Maybe for the sake of my stomach if nothing else no other reason.

The next time I stopped by the smithy, which, of course, I did a few days later, he was supervising a younger boy who was repairing a small table. He noticed me standing with my errand basket held tightly this time and came to me.

"So, Gabriella, have you managed to avoid a mauling while collecting your eggs?" I took his mocking tone as a challenge.

"I will get the hang of it. I need to let these hens know who is their master and they will be fine."

He laughed. "I understand you play the violin beautifully." He walked closer, just two feet from me, and leaned upon the wall of the smithy. This time he was dressed in gray work pants and work shirt I noticed with a little disappointment.

"You, sir, are sadly misinformed," I said.

"Do you like it here, countess? It is hardly a fine estate and must be very different from your previous life."

He was well spoken, I noticed, and must have received some education. "It is my life now whether it matters or not. I will make of it all I can. What do you know of me and my former life?"

"The Ospedale is a little town within a town. Any new arrival is much discussed. Especially one with so... much talent. His gaze swept over my figure and then his dark blue eyes looked deeply into my own. I felt myself blushing. This man wore no priest's collar to dissuade me. I made a clumsy excuse and fled.

I continued on to my next task with fierce determination to let no man distract me. The day was full, and I thought nothing of this fateful meeting until that night, when I lay alone in my bed, troubled and excited. I closed my eyes. After saying my nightly prayers to protect and keep my mother, father, and little brothers, I thought of Raphael. The pictures in the large leather book in my father's library came to my mind. Once again, I found it hard to sleep for obvious and sinful reasons.

The next morning I got up early and found Veronica tuning her violin in the parlor between our rooms. I told her of my discovery.

"Oh, you have met our Raphael! He does appreciate a pretty face and ample bosoms. In the past he has shown a preference for brunettes, but he is always attracted to the novel."

"Tell me of him." I sat on the bench next to her and she gave me a stern look; I had interrupted her while tuning. She tuned each string meticulously each morning as naturally as she brushed her hair. She and the instrument were one.

Now she returned to her task but went on talking. "Raphael is the bastard son of a king and demands to be treated as such. He is an excellent lover." She glanced up and gave me a curious look. "Such things can be arranged if you are interested."

My cheeks burned. Having no right to care about "such things."

Still I could not help it. I had told Veronica about Antonio.

She knew how "such things" had led to my ruin. I had once opened my heart to her, and I reminded her of that now.

Veronica laughed. "As I have said, there are ways to keep love from resulting in a child. I am, after all, the daughter of a courtesan. Such an upbringing comes with special knowledge."

I was interested and repulsed at once. "I have promised myself that the act of physical love would not be a casual matter to me again," I said to her.

"Suit yourself."

This time, she laid her violin down and gave me her full attention. "The nights get long and lonely here. There are worse diversions than passing the hours in the arms of a handsome and willing lover. You could grow old waiting for some patron to notice you at a concert and ask for your hand in marriage. "

"What! This can happen? One can find a patron and be allowed to marry?" But my father had mentioned that possibility. How could I have forgotten? Perhaps when my father said it, I had been too distraught to understand; I had assumed that this school would be my life until I dropped dead at the keyboard like my predecessor. My heart leapt and Veronica saw this on my face.

"Don't be so quick to wish yourself away from here. Life in the world can be cruel." Veronica looked out her window and I could see sadness in those beautiful sapphire eyes. But there was no time to ask questions. We were late for morning prayers as usual.

CHAPTER TWELVE

My days were full and passed quickly. Not so the nights. The ache in my heart for my mother's soft hand upon my face before I fell asleep, or the look of love in my father's eyes as I played a piece just for him, kept me awake. I even missed my little brothers' racing into my room uninvited. I often found myself pacing in my chamber after Veronica returned to her room.

I longed for all that I had lost. It still hurt too much to even think of my child, and I felt empty. My life had purpose but, still selfishly, I wanted more. I have mentioned desire that sometimes bubbled up within me, but there was a greater hunger deep in my heart. I longed to be close to someone, as my mother and father were close. I longed for love. The possibility of marriage Veronica had mentioned filled me with hope. But hope did not hold me close in the dark, so I paced.

I would not, I decided, be as a piece of silk in the wind. I would take charge of my life, find a suitable patron and marry him. There would be more to my life than music lessons and errands. I need not waste away in this school. I would not be denied the life I deserved because of one afternoon with a stable hand.

One fine warm morning, the thin old nun who had attended me during my recovery came to see me before breakfast in my room. Remembering her kindness during my convalescence, I was glad to see her again.

"I am Sister Maria," she said, taking my hand. "It is time for you to visit the Garden of Innocents. You have regained your strength. Now you need to see where he lies." Her smile held only kindness within the deep wrinkled valleys of her face.

I knew I must go, but this was a day I had hoped would never come.

"We will leave for San Michele right after breakfast," said Sister Maria and then she vanished down the hall.

San Michele, I knew, was the island of the dead. Venice was a collection of tiny islands in a vast lagoon; there was little room for the dead to lie in peace. I felt as cold and gray inside as this raw day the sister had chosen for my duty to be done. The sky looked as if it would pour rain at any moment. As the oarsman rowed us to the island, I saw a cold gray rock surrounded by a high stone wall. It was a bleak impression, and my heart ached at the thought of my child sleeping on this desolate rock forever.

We climbed out of the boat and I followed Sister Maria as she climbed the stairs. I saw that this island was not a barren gray rock after all. The trees were not tall and so could not be seen from the water below. San Michel was covered with small trees and shrubs. They were spring-flowering trees and at this time of year were covered with buds, some already bursting into blooms.

"The island is a riot of color most of the year," Sister Maria said. "I wanted to bring you later in the spring when the flowers are in full bloom, but Lent fast approaches and the Ospedale will begin preparations for Easter soon."

She moved quickly for her age and we stopped under a tree thick with fat white buds whose branches spread as if to protect a small, fenced yard. A sign on the fence read, "Garden of the Innocents. Rest Well, Little Lambs." A statue of a lamb stood at the entrance of the stone fence as if on guard. Inside the fence were dozens of tiny crosses of white-washed wood no taller than a foot. Each cross looked identical to the one next to it except for a number on each. The good sister knew which one was his. I was determined not to cry. Tears would change nothing. He deserved my courage to honor him.

Sister Maria walked to the end of the last row and stopped at a cross with the number 728 carved on it. How fitting that this was the number of the page on which I had discovered the "Gates of Heaven" in my father's library. This made me smile a little. My babe was surely within the gates of Heaven now.

Even in such a sad place, I could see he rested well. The wise sister walked a few paces away, giving me some time to pray alone. On my knees beside his grave, I thanked God for the beautiful place for my babe to rest. I thanked God for the peace of my new life. I would never forget the loss of my child but living a life of grief would not bring him back. Perhaps with God's great grace someday... I rose from my knees and walked back to the little red boat where the oarsman waited.

On our walk back, I said nothing for a while. And then my natural inclination toward conversation took over. "Sister, please tell me more about the Garden of the Innocents. Who are they and where do they all come from?"

"Well," she began as the man rowed us back to our home. "Their number is now fifty-five in this new portion of the garden, which is five years in the making. The total for all the years is hundreds."

More than seven hundred, I thought to myself. And I knew but one of the sad little stories that must accompany each small cross.

"It is the curse," the Sister said. "It has resumed its cruel punishment of the Ospedale. All those babes were born before their time, and praise to the Holy Mother, all were baptized before being lain to rest in this hallowed ground. So many have been lost these last five years. We used to have many little babes in our nursery, but now it lies empty. The orphan babies dropped off at the little window are sent to our sister convent in Verona, as there are no others here now for them to play with. When they are six, they come back to us. Only the little ones born here are allowed to stay, but now...." Her voice trailed. She was silent for a long while, and though she looked away, I saw tears in her eyes.

"I do so miss the littlest ones. They were my special mission for many years. Now I visit them here, far too often and attend to the girls about to give birth."

"All were born too soon?" I ask.

She didn't answer at once but looked as if she longed to tell me something she should not. At last she said, "It is the Curse."

"Please, I must know of this curse," I pleaded.

She put her head close to mine and spoke softly, though there was no one but the boatman in earshot, and he had his hands full. I had to strain to hear over the sound of the waves.

"Tell no one we spoke of this. The headmistress forbids such talk." I nodded, and she went on. "Many years ago, the Ospedale served as a hostel for crusaders bound for the Holy land. A small group of nuns saw to the needs of the soldiers on their pilgrimage. In those days, most of the sisters were young, as the Ospedale was newly built and staffed. The crusaders, though on a holy mission, were men still and acted as men do. One of the youngest sisters, Angelica by name, fell in love. The knight whom she loved went off to do his duty, leaving Sister Angelica behind and with child. The sister was little more than a child herself. Pregnancy, desertion, and shame caused her to become unbalanced in her mind. Each day as her belly grew, the sister went to the top of the little tower at the back gate, watching in vain for her knight to return. On the day the child was born, she climbed the tower once again with the newborn girl in her arms." The old nun crossed herself. "She jumped from the tower with the babe still in her arms. Some said in her weakened state she fell, but all knew of her tragic and mortal sin. Because of that sin, it is said, God cursed the Ospedale and reclaims for himself all babes that are born here.

After a long pause followed by a sigh, she said. "I have been here all my life. I am proof that at one time the curse seemed to have left us. My mother gave birth to me at the Ospedale. When I lived, all the sisters hoped that God had relented. We were shocked as five years ago his wrath began anew with Veronica's babe, the first to be buried in the new section in the Garden of Innocents." The shock and horror of this revelation must have shown on my face, for the kind Sister took my hand. "Yes, our own dear Veronica. She could have been no more than twelve years old when it happened."

No wonder that beautiful face was sometimes marred by sadness, I thought.

"Remember well," the nun said, "but speak to no one of this."

Some days later the weather turned warm once more and I sat upon my bed longing for home and my old life once more. Veronica appeared in my doorway and could see the melancholy on my face. She seemed to feel for me and sought to lift my darkness.

"Have you never seen the contemplation garden behind the chapel?" said Veronica from my doorway. She came into my room and stood next to me. "It is so lovely this time of year." She opened my wardrobe.

"Why don't you put on one of these lovely gowns. Nothing can lift one's spirits like wearing something pretty. Our drab work clothes depress me." She turned the corners of her mouth down and I laughed.

"Here," said Veronica, taking a particularly pretty gown off the hanger. "This green velvet would suit you so well." It was a deep green mantua that matched my eyes. The sleeves were slit to reveal satin of the same color. A slit down the front of the skirt displayed exquisite ruffles of deep green satin.

"Oh, do put in on. I would love to see it on you." Veronica handed the gown to me, smiling as brightly as I had ever seen. She helped me to lace up the back, and I looked in the mirror. There I saw the Gabriella of old wearing only the loveliest gowns without a care in the world. I could not help but smile.

"If I did not have to practice soon, I would put on my prettiest gown, though I have nothing to compare, and we would go enjoy the flowers in the contemplation garden and dazzle those blossoms with our beauty."

The idea appealed to me.

"Go, Gabriella. Wear that gown and visit that lovely spot. You deserve to leave your cares and sadness behind for a little while. Perhaps I can finish my practice early and will join you." She looked at me with raised eyebrows.

"I will. Thank you for the wonderful idea." She told me how to move the old shrubs aside on the right side of the chapel and assured me I would have the garden to myself at this time of day.

The sun shone brightly, and I was relieved that no one seemed to notice me or my unusually formal dress as I crossed the rectangular courtyard to the chapel. I found the private garden easily and seated myself on the little stone bench Veronica told me of. Tiny blue periwinkle peeked out at the foot of fragrant lilacs as if approving of my attire.

I sat lost in happy memories of home when a shadow fell on the flowers in front of me. I looked up at Raphael standing close by. He was completely dressed in an elegant, black velvet coat with gold buttons and matching britches. His spotless white hose caressed his well-muscled calves. His wild hair had been attended to and gleamed golden in the dappled light. He smiled down at me. Without invitation, he sat down on the bench, so close I could feel the warmth of his leg through our clothes.

"Good afternoon, Gabriella," he said. "How lovely to find you dressed in such finery. Is it for me, this lovely change?" He looked me up and down slowly as if I were a cream filled pastry.

I had opened my mouth to correct this fallacy when, to my great surprise, he covered my mouth with a kiss. I did not rebuff him immediately. Finally, my dormant sense of decency intervened, and I pulled away. I could hear my rapid breathing, and so could he. He leaned closer to kiss me once again, and this time he caressed my breast through the fabric of my gown.

Feelings stirred in me, low feelings; but I put my hands to his chest and pushed him away. "Sir, you mistake me. I came here for solitude."

"You toy with me, my lovely. Well, I like a good game." He cocked his head slightly. "There can be great pleasure in the chase. To find a beautiful lady so finely gowned for my pleasure, in such a secluded place, is a game I am sure to enjoy." Raphael took my hand. I thought he meant to kiss it. This would not have been entirely improper in another place, and I admit I let him. Instead, he turned my hand over and slowly ran his warm tongue along my palm, lingering at last between my fingers. I felt a stirring in a place that a true and virtuous lady would never mention, but I was shocked. I gasped and pulled away.

He dropped my hand with a look of surprise. "I am sorry. Veronica assured me this was also your desire,"

"Veronica! How could she!" I cried. Then I gathered my skirts and beat a hasty and ungraceful retreat to my room.

Even as my color returned to normal, my breathing slowed, and I changed into my plain muslin work clothes; I had but one thought: Veronica! She would answer for this humiliation.

I went at once to the room where she taught violin at this time of day. I opened the door and saw twenty little girls, none older that eight, playing a pretty violin concerto with far more skill than I could ever manage. I stood at the back of the room, glaring, until she released her little pupils early. "Hello, Gabriella. Mary Elise has mastered this piece nicely, don't you think?" she said as the girls filed out. "Should I ask her to give you a lesson? She is nearly seven, after all."

I marched to the front of the class and grabbed her arm. "We need to talk alone, now."

Her eyes widened in alarm. My temper flared; I would have dragged her to the little instrument storage room next door if she had not come willingly. But she came without protest, looking concerned and puzzled.

I closed the door. "What did you say to Raphael that led him to accost me behind the chapel?" With each word my voice became louder and by the last one I was shouting.

At first, Veronica looked contrite. "I know you admire him, and he spends far too much time with courtesans these days. He tells me he is quite enamored of your beauty. I thought a little tryst was something you would both enjoy."

I didn't answer. As I seethed with silent rage, she continued. "He has worked hard to gain his position of responsibility at the Ospedale. Although Raphael is a bastard, he strives to earn a place in decent society. He deserves better than the shallow courtesans that take all of his money. And you— I hear how you pace at night." Veronica's tone changed to one I had heard from her before, instructing a dull student.

"I thought," she said, "that you might enjoy the attentions of a gentleman rather than a stable boy."

I had never hit anyone in my life. I had once nearly slit a man's throat, as you remember, but that was self-defense. I had to stop myself then from slapping the false smile from Veronica's face. Holding my arm tight to my side, I said, "You know what such casual passion has cost me. How could you think I would enjoy such a thing!"

"I told you there are ways to prevent accidents," Veronica said smugly, with maddening calm. "Raphael would certainly know of those ways."

"I didn't bury an *accident*. I buried my child. You should of all people know this pain too well."

These words evoked an even colder smile. "I am sorry if my little arrangement caused you distress."

It was in this moment our friendship changed forever. I saw that she did not possess the capacity to feel for others. Something was broken inside of her. Most of my anger faded with this tragic realization. I could not help pitying the beautiful girl whose heart was encased forever in ice. Though we would remain cordial, I lost my closest friend that day. I could never again trust her with my deepest secrets or give her access to my heart. Such trust might well have saved my life.

CHAPTER THIRTEEN

Just as many times before and since, when troubled, I buried myself in music. I tutored girls who needed extra help and in my free time, I practiced incessantly. Easter was coming and a great performance would take place. I was to play a solo, my first since I came to the Ospedale.

As I practiced my pianoforte one afternoon, I felt someone standing over my left shoulder. Turning my head, I saw the Red Priest intently watched my play with a smile. I could not help but blush.

"I have something for you, Gabriella. Something I think you will like," he said. I got up from my bench as to face him respectfully. He gave me sheets of music, not written in his hand. The notes were tiny and extremely neat. "There is a young church organist from Leipzig who writes beautifully for keyboards. I wish you to help me arrange his work for you to perform on Easter."

"Thank you, Father," I said in astonishment. His handsome brow creased, and he sat down upon the harpsichord bench.

"Please, don't call me that. My name is Antonio." His head sank into his hands.

Of course, I could not call the maestro by his Christian name. I may have done many unseemly things in my life, but this would not be one more of them.

"Enough about me, lovely child. I came to talk of music.

Herr Bach wrote to me of his admiration for my work. In appreciation, he sent me the work you hold in your hand. Tell me what you think."

I sat down on the bench and played the first page. When I raised my eyes, I saw that while he waited patiently, the maestro's eyes never left me.

"It is beautiful. I hope I can do it justice," I said.

"Let there be no false modesty between us, Gabriella." The soft way he said my name hid grievous danger to my soul. "No other girl at the Ospedale can compare to your talent at the keyboard, or your beauty."

My cheeks colored and my heart quickened slightly. His generous compliment led to thoughts I should not have dared. I have committed many sins in my brief life. I did not intend at that moment to damn my soul to hell for impure thoughts of a priest, for this handsome, masterful genius of a man was still a priest. I vowed to keep my eyes on the pianoforte and the music for the rest of the session. At last, after an hour or so, one of the old priests came to fetch the maestro.

I felt relief at his leaving and I am certain it showed on my face. The maestro turned back to me and said, "Remember that name, Johannes Bach. I think this German organist has promise. Your playing will do his music a service. This may be the first it has been played in all of Venice. I doubt it will be the last."

I have tried to change my sinful ways, and my hanging will end my sinning. It may help my soul in the next life if I admit them all. And so I tell you, in my room at night my thoughts of the maestro added blasphemy to my list of sins. Try as I might, I could not stop those thoughts. His rich dark red hair, wide shoulders, warm, brown eyes...and the thought of what lay beneath his cassock. May God have mercy on my immortal soul. Pray for me, friends, when I am swinging from a rope.

I shiver at the thought, though the day is warm.

My sessions with the maestro became the focus of my life. Even so, my days felt empty as I missed my friend Veronica. We passed each other in the classrooms or the halls and merely nodded. Gone were our whispered talks long after the order came to snuff the candles. I was left alone at night with my unholy thoughts of priests and the premature deaths of infants.

Raphael I avoided at all cost. My goal now was to find a suitable husband from the concert patrons, and the Easter Concert presented a perfect opportunity. Surely this goal must distract me from my thoughts of the maestro.

Often, out of loneliness, I sought the company of my students, some of whom were older than I, and conversing with them helped to pass the time until I could practice. One day, as one of the more garrulous of my students took her lesson, I tried gently to get some answers to questions that troubled me.

"Have you ever heard old sister Maria speak of a curse on the Ospedale?" I asked, as lightly as I could when speaking of such a dark subject.

Maria Helena was gaining little benefit that day from my teaching, I'm afraid. The good-natured kitchen girl's playing was hindered by the thickness of her fingers; too much tasting, perhaps. She was happy to take a break from banging on my favorite instrument and seemed excited at the mention of this forbidden topic.

"Oh yes." Her round face lit up. "We all know about it. One more little cross has been added to the Garden in the last month." She looked around behind her to insure no one else was near enough to hear. "Natalia was found to be with child, though no one knew, she being such a large girl and looking much the same before as after."

"I knew nothing of her sorrow," I said. "She seems to be recovering well. I saw her yesterday, and she bore not a sign."

"Yes, she is not very bright, and seems not to care about her loss. This is not the first time she has been with child and been delivered too soon. No one knows who the father was, but Natalia is always where she should not be and is unduly friendly with the day laborers who sometimes work for our Overseer." The mention of Raphael gave me a tiny shudder of regret.

I put my hand upon her shoulder and the scent of onions and browned meat fat wafted up. "We must never speak of this."

"Oh, of course not." She smiled, raised herself off the piano bench and left the practice room.

One more cross. How could this be happening? This could not be the work of any curse or the will of God. The God that created music and life could never do such a thing and I do not believe in curses. Some mortal must be responsible. Why would anyone want to end such innocent lives before they began? Why would anyone want to do such a terrible and evil thing? If one did harbor such evil desires, how could this be done? Whom could I ask?

When I arrived at the music room for my lesson with the maestro, I found another lesson still in progress. Veronica was just finishing a lovely sonata written by the maestro himself. Though I had not heard it before, his beautifully light and happy style was unmistakable. Hesitating to go in, I stood in the back of the room in the shadows to watch. Veronica finished and put her violin in its case. "Good enough, Antonio?" Her familiar use of his Christian name irritated me.

"No other girl here is your equal." The maestro gazed at her with adoration and bent close. I thought he meant to kiss her, but he merely picked up the music she had been playing and said, "Now, my lovely winter's girl, I have another lesson to give." The look Veronica gave Maestro Vivaldi could only be described as wanton. He did not look away.

"There is no time today for more?" Veronica said, looking up at him.

He laughed. "I will not forget that winter is the most dangerous of all the seasons. We must save something for another day."

His tone was intimate. I realized the feeling deep within me was not merely righteous condemnation, but jealousy. This feeling was as improper and ridiculous as it was strong and real. I ignored it and told myself that if Veronica wanted to send her soul to hell, so be it. Mine would not follow.

I could not resist slipping out of the room and re-entering

with a heavy step. I gave Veronica the coldest smile I could muster. Compared to the one I received in return, mine was warm as the summer sun. She picked up her violin and music and as she made to leave, she turned to the maestro and said, "Tomorrow, Antonio?" He answered with a nod, nothing more, yet their shared air of familiarity disturbed me to my core. How dare she call the maestro simply Antonio? I placed my music on the pianoforte with a loud thump and sat down on the bench.

"Is something wrong, Gabriella?" Maestro Vivaldi inquired with what seemed genuine concern.

"I do not think it proper to call one's superior by his Christian name." These words sounded as bitter and jealous as in truth they were. I longed to take them back as soon as they left my lips. Maestro Vivaldi laughed the deep music that was his laugh, as if to dismiss such silly feelings.

"I offered you the same privilege, do you not remember?" I met his eyes.

"The way Veronica spoke to you was not decent."

He returned my look directly. "There is no decent or indecent between us. There is only the passion for the music and its beauty. Your passion makes your playing even more magnificent." He reached over and put his hand on my keyboard. "The pianoforte is an instrument that lends itself to the passionate, perhaps more than any other. Thank you, my golden girl for the inspiration." I smiled a small smile at his words.

"I do not envy Herr Bach. He has only a church congregation to inspire him. I have the inspiration of all the passing seasons of young womanhood. Herr Bach composes works of great beauty with his little inspiration. I am lazy and compose only when required. Perhaps I enjoy my inspiration too much."

The sadness in those words gave me a courage that may surprise even the boldest of you. I reached over, took his hand, and pressed it to my breast. Wrong, of course, yet I swear I meant it as a gesture of compassion. I felt no shame.

He did not pull his hand away. Sighing deeply, he said, "I am afraid, Gabriella, inspiration is all I can ever take from such great beauty as yours. I dropped his hand as if it was a burning coal from the fires of hell.

He laughed and said, "Do not feel ashamed. It is I who am to blame for your innocent attentions."

"My feelings for you are far from innocent." Though I knew well how wrong this was, I could not stop myself.

He took my hand in his. "Mine is the greatest sin. I encourage your feelings and use them to fuel the music I write. I see the admiration on your beautiful young faces, and though my sin is surely a dark one, I do not discourage you. It inspires me. That is why we have such greatness here. Forgive me, I cannot help myself." He walked to the window and looked out. "In truth, I do not wish to help myself. I am punished now in life, as I may be in the fires of eternal damnation. Can you, Gabriella, imagine a starving man forced always to smell delicious food while having vowed to taste not one single bite? I draw strength from this, my hunger." He turned back to face me, amusement in his eyes.

"Now turn your eyes to that keyboard, my little petit four, and play. We have only four more days until our most holy savior's rising."

I played for him then as I never had before, with a passion and mastery I hadn't known I possessed. It was clear that he expected nothing less.

CHAPTER FOURTEEN

An abundance of activity engulfed the Ospedale as the Easter season approached. Every classroom and chamber was broomed to perfect cleanliness and special treats were prepared to end Lent's long season of praying and denial. Every stick of wood that made up the grand Concert Hall was oiled and polished to perfection. Even the stained glass was cleaned and polished to let in more light for our savior's rising. Many extra hours were added to our daily chores. My skill with the broom was improving, and I became nearly as good at polishing wood as I was at instructing others how to do it.

The Easter performance was like no other. All the girls to perform were dressed in their finest, some borrowed, some purchased just for this concert. I shared several of my best things with anyone whom they fit. Girls piled their hair high upon their heads, powdered their faces and even rouged their cheeks. Some of the bolder girls dared to powder their shiny hair, which was the new fashion. I did not want my hair powdered. I was proud of my golden mane.

I look down at the crowd assembled below me. "Please forgive my vanity and do not think less of me. I have so little time left. I heard someone say my death waits only for the hangman who has been delayed. It cannot be long now." I catch the eye of the young blacksmith and say, "Thank you, Marco, for the wine that cools my parched throat and gives courage to my tongue. I am grateful for anything that will ease my way out of this life."

"I heard a rumor," said Marco, looking up at me, "that the hangman has disappeared and a new one must be found. Maybe you will have time to finish your story after all."

I pour another cup, give him a kind smile, and I continue.

Our performance to honor our savior's resurrection was a very public one. All our weekly evening performances were open to the public, but most nights there were but few faithful patrons in attendance, hidden from us by a wooden screen. One could not know who watched as we played each night. But this night we performed in the front of the hall with nothing between the audience and we the orchestra.

"You will not believe the finery of the patrons gathered," said a girl somewhere in the row behind me as we stood in a line ready to take our seats.

"Perhaps there is a wealthy man sitting in the crowd who wants the very best recorder player for a wife," said another girl whose voice I did not recognize as we waited to play.

"That would not be you, Elizabetta," said someone, and everyone laughed.

On this Easter evening, the gallery was so full that extra chairs were placed in many rows in the concert hall. It appeared the money allotted for a year's-worth of candles had been spent on this one night. The candles in each large candelabra were not the usual dim and smoky tallow but were the finest bee's wax. The room was bright with all manner of loveliness. It shone with the beauty of the music and the lovely girls that played it.

Maestro Vivaldi's position as Maestro d'Concerti required an Easter composition each year and this year, that commission was wonderfully fulfilled. This orchestra of talented girls did his work justice. Every note, if not perfect, was covered by the passion of the maestro's brilliant writing and conducting.

As Maestro Vivaldi's conducting was chiefly concluded, I put down my hautboy, walked between the other members of the group, and quickly took my place at the pianoforte for the grand finale. I was to play the work of Johann Sebastian Bach. The maestro, magnificent in his wig and Easter vestment of pure white satin trimmed in gold, told the large audience of the work and its significance. "Our soloist will be Maria Gabriella Constanzi Pompeii, our beloved keyboard teacher." The other girls clapped wildly. The audience was merely polite. Perhaps my future husband would be in that audience, I thought, my mouth as dry as dust from the deepest corners of the crypt below the chapel.

Maestro Antonio, as I would allow myself to call him only in my heart, walked over to my pianoforte and the look he gave me erased all my doubt. I played the young German organist's music as I had never played any piece. At that moment, I so love the exact nature of the piano. Each note is precisely where it should be. Each time you touch the keys, you may vary the pressure or the tempo, but the precision of the note is always there for you in its proper place.

My fingers flew as if they had wings. The hours of practice under the maestro's watch, filled with helpful suggestions, allowed me to translate the joy and the beauty of the music clearly and purely as I had only dreamed in the past. When finished, my play was met with silence. Had I imagined the quality of my play? But even as that fear set in, the crowd erupted in thunderous applause that went on and on. Standing, I humbly bowed.

I glanced at our orchestra and all the girls were smiling, save one. Veronica's solo had been the highlight of the evening until I played the Bach. I must admit, a tear ran down my cheek as she played. Not just for the sadness I felt for my inadequacy, but honest appreciation for the beauty she wrought from the beautiful and terrible violin. Veronica had been magnificent.

When I finished my piece, she gave me a look with not her usual cold falseness, but one filled with anger and envy rivaling the liquid rock from Vesuvius. Then, even as I returned her look with one of triumph and pure joy, she had reverted to her usual frozen countenance. Veronica, ever the ice queen of deepest winter: I could not help but pity her, but I had won this contest for the heart of the audience. There was no fire hot enough to warm her cold heart and in it, no room for anyone else.

After my bow, the audience demanded another, and another until my modesty forbade any more. Still, they clapped and cheered until we left the stage.

We gathered in the narrow hall behind the great concert chamber. A reception would take place in the Concert hall for the patrons and we were generously allowed to attend. Everywhere, girls of all ages fussed with their hair, straightened gowns, and pinched or rouged cheeks in anticipation of this reception. All were invited. Patrons who had given large sums of money to support the Ospedale wished to speak to the recipients of their largesse. Most of the girls just wanted to show off their dresses and talk to the well-dressed and interesting patrons.

I stood up straight to accent my attributes and unleashed my smile. I stopped just long enough to arrange the curls that I wore long and loose, checking myself in the small mirror someone had brought. Then I followed the line of girls out into the concert hall.

All of our instruments and most of the chairs had been removed. Tables were set up in the middle of the room. Bottles of wine were poured into crystal glasses by some of the older nuns, who stood by with steady hands and watchful eyes. People wrapped in finery milled around drinking wine, conversing and laughing. We girls had been instructed that only one glass of wine was proper; after that we must excuse ourselves and go to our rooms. I intended to make my one glass of wine last for hours.

As I passed through the small crowd, I received smiles and nods of approval. One beautifully dressed lady thanked me for the beauty of my performance. She dropped me a little curtsey of gratitude, holding her skirt of pale gray velvet embroidered with gold and silver spangles. I returned her a grateful curtsy, so that she might see my good breeding, and engaged her in conversation for as long as seemed proper. Such a lady may have a brother or a son in search of a wife.

Still smiling, I was heading to the refreshment table when I saw him. My breath caught in my throat. Raphael stood in a corner leaning against the wall, wearing a deep red brocade coat, black britches and a dangerous smile. Warmth flooded my cheeks, and as I turned on my heels, I heard him laugh long and loud. I stopped in my tracks. I was no coward to run from a man. If there was to be laughter, I preferred to share in it.

I turned around and headed toward him, returning his smile with one of my own that was brilliant, if not entirely genuine. With a look of surprise on his handsome face, he took his foot off the wall and stood up, smoothing his coat. "I have come to apologize for my unforgivable behavior behind the chapel," he said with a deep bow. "Can you ever forgive me?"

"It is already done." I said. "You had no more fault than I." No woman could have resisted the truly repentant and totally charming look in those blue eyes.

"I have two additional things to say to you, Gabriella. First, I have rarely listened to the music with much attention, but your performance was magnificent. Second, why have you been avoiding me? I have watched as you take the longest way around me each day."

"I was too embarrassed to face you. After what Veronica told you. I was sure you must think me a harlot or at least a fool."

"I think of you only with fondness." He took a small step toward me, a hungry look on his face. "Veronica told me of your talent and you have just proved the truth of this to me. Your beauty I could always see for myself." He handed me a glass of wine, and we stood talking as I took the tiniest sips.

"So tell me, Gabriella, have you learned to collect the eggs without feathers flying and blood dripping?"

"Those chickens are the bane of my existence. I cannot understand how anyone could handle such evil monsters."

"Have you thought of consulting an expert? Perhaps the person that did the task before you?"

"That would be ridiculous. Marietta collected the eggs before I came and she has the intelligence of a hen herself." I took a sip and glared at him.

"Cannot expertise come from experience and not merely intelligence?"

I smiled and nodded but paid little attention to the conversation; I was busy drinking in this handsome man who thought me beautiful. The time came when I looked sadly into the bottom of my glass. "My wine is finished. I must go back to my room, on orders of the headmistress."

"May I walk with you?" Then, seeing my look, he said, "I mean nothing lascivious. I am just not ready to relinquish the pleasure of your company." In his expression, I saw nothing but sincerity.

"I would like that. I must warn you Sister Theresa is known as 'Sister Sleepless'." She oversees our quarters and would beat any man to death with her broom who dared try to enter." This picture created in my head made me laugh and Raphael joined me in this small amusement.

Leaving the concert hall, we walked slowly back to the building that housed my room. He walked so close that it was hard for me to think clearly. "How is it you attend the Patron's reception?" I asked.

"Well, I am, of course, exceedingly wealthy and have donated many fine instruments to the Ospedale." He looked at me sideways and we both laughed. "I am allowed because of my position to attend all the functions. I come to evening concerts when I have nothing better to attend."

"You are truly a music lover, then. Do you play?" I asked.

"Sadly no, I have as much music in these hands as any smith in my employ. No, I mainly come to see the girls. Until your solo tonight, I had only imagined that anyone could play as you do." He had stopped in his tracks and turned to me. "Veronica told me you were exceptional, but I had no idea how right she was. As you know, she is not always totally truthful."

I turned to Raphael in sudden irritation. "Do you prize the opinions of all your lovers so highly?"

He seemed shocked. "Veronica is not my lover. She never could be."

"She is beautiful and immensely talented as well. From what you have said, that is very much to your taste."

"Veronica is both of those things I admire, but she could

never be my lover. Veronica is my sister."

Why had I not noticed his dark blue eyes were exactly the same shade of deep sapphire as Veronica's? How could I not have suspected this link? I hid my shock at his revelation and walked on.

He went on to tell me of their birth to a favored courtesan. "There were three of us 'accidents of love,' as my mother often called us. I am the oldest. Then there is my brother Anton, two years younger, and Veronica, who was born when I was twelve. I have not seen my brother since he left to work on a country estate far from Venice years ago. I never knew exactly why our mother kept me with her. It must have been that my considerable charm was evident even as a child." He gave me another sly glance and continued. "It is not desirable for courtesans to have little children hanging on their satin skirts or disarranging their perfumed hair.

"My mother was the best of courtesans and her only real interest was being attractive to her clients. It killed her. She died of the French Pox, undoubtedly contracted from a patron. It is the most common cause of death for women of her profession. Don't blame Veronica," he said. "She was merely trying to help us both. I had confessed to her that I had noticed her new friend and wished to know her better."

"She has made such arrangements for you previously?" I asked, though I did not really want to hear the answer.

"Alas, yes... She loves me in her way. Veronica never realizes that such arrangements, though briefly satisfying, may not be what I really need. I admit I am not innocent in my participation. I am just a man." He took a few steps and began again.

"Not all the girls here have your high moral standards, Gabriella. My mother made her living from the pleasures of the flesh; I myself give in too often to temptation." The little smile he gave me was at once sad and threatening to my virtue. It was dangerous to feel anything for this admitted rake. It was unwise; but I could not resist feeling something for Raphael at that moment, too much for my own good.

Our path had led us to the door to my dormitory. As I turned to say goodbye, I noticed Sister Theresa just inside the door, broom in hand. He wanted to kiss me, I could feel it, but perhaps he saw her too, for he merely smiled, bowed, and backed away into the dark courtyard.

I went to my room, wishing the good sister had gone to bed a little earlier that night.

I lay awake for hours with the excitement of all the evening had wrought. I had enjoyed my performance immensely and been well rewarded with cheers and applause. I had learned something about Veronica that evening, which caused me to reconsider our severed friendship. She'd acted out of love for her brother. Perhaps she was capable of caring for someone else after all.

I was also glad that Raphael and I were friendly once again. In my deepest heart, did I want much more than his friendship? Yet Raphael had distracted me from my task. I'd spent my time on him and thus met no suitable patrons. I spent hours dreaming when I needed to investigate this supposed curse. Still, I told myself, there would be other concerts on the horizon, and I allowed myself to think of Raphael's outrageously blue eyes.

At last I gave up on sleep and rose to watch the courtyard out my window. It was a serene view on most nights, but on this night I was amazed at the comings and goings. At all hours, dark figures crossed to and fro. Who were they and where were they going? Sometimes I could recognize the shadow figures. Sister Maria, though old and thin, moved with amazing speed, crossing from the convent to the infirmary to tend the sick even in the middle of the night. The Head Mistress, Sister Angelica, was built like a barrel and waddled as she walked heading to the kitchen at this late hour. Others moved furtively, seeming to appreciate the cover of darkness.

The greatest number of the shadowy figures by far came from the common girls' dormitory. Sometimes, I would watch as the figures disappeared out the main gate and did not return while I was awake. Often I would see two figures meet and head off close together. Arrangements had certainly been made.

CHAPTER FIFTEEN

In the daylight, I filled my hours with lessons and errands and held my plan for a new future in my heart. Some days, however, I could not help seeking flavor for this stew of my Ospedale life. I would find out where Raphael was working and would plant myself there. I tried to look fetching and always wear a smile. Not a difficult thing to do when I thought of Raphael. I was grateful someone always knew where he was, so important to the Ospedale's functioning was our overseer. Late one morning, I managed to cross his path as he delivered a large pot that had been repaired to the kitchen. He stopped to wish me good morning, and I grew bold.

"I have a bit of cold chicken and would share it, if you would like to take your noon meal with me in the lovely spot beside the seawall," I said. This message was conveyed with the sweetest smile and flutter of eyelashes.

"Did you cook up one of the vile beasts who gored you?

"Perhaps." I held up the basket of food. "You see what becomes of those who displease me."

Raphael laughed and agreed to take the risk to eat with me. I was so happy to think of spending time with him that I nearly gave my heart's desire away that very minute. But if the truth be told, it may have been already given at the Easter concert, no matter my plans.

The garden behind the chapel held only remembered feelings of shame. The little spot I chose for our meeting was protected by the seawall near the old guard tower. Though no one had stood guard since the Crusades, the tower, now overgrown with vines, provided shade in this hot part of the day.

I spread a cloth on the ground in the shadow of the ruined tower. This spot could be seen from several angles and so I thought it a proper choice. Glimpses of Raphael about his duties always raised the color in my cheeks, but today, I could hardly catch my breath as I watched him walk toward me. I could see he had stopped to change his shirt, but on that hot day, beads of sweat trickled down his neck. Like the lady I am no longer, I looked away and set out cold chicken, bread and some olives I had managed to pry loose from the kitchen.

He gave me a quick peck on my cheek and sat beside me. As we ate, we spoke of the continued hot spell and the delivery of new poultry, but Raphael seemed distracted. His brow furrowed, he grew quiet.

Some minutes passed, and I had to ask him. "What is the matter, your thoughts seem to be elsewhere?"

"There are things women need not concern themselves with in this world," he said.

"Is not half of this world filled with women?" I asked.

"Well, I suppose so."

"Then why should we not concern ourselves with all the world contains? All this world concerns women. A man who is not intelligent enough to know this will never amount to anything."

He turned his head to look at me with narrowed eyes, but he did not speak a word.

I still felt the need to educate him on the value of women and continued my rant. "My father and my mother were partners in life and it brought out the best in both of them. He would have been much less without her and she without him." I spoke boldly and with all the conviction I had inside me.

He studied my face and his gaze softened. "If I had not wanted to be challenged, I should have chosen another girl to dine with. There are many here, almost as pretty, that are much more willing and agreeable and I doubt any of the other girls would instruct me on exactly how to kiss them."

I opened my mouth to protest, but his look reassured me of the jest. He reached over and took my hand, this time chaste and respectful. "Alas, I no longer have much choice. I am afraid that you may be stealing my heart, Gabriella."

He ceased to talk and kissed me properly. His lips were soft, and I parted mine slightly. He gently teased my tongue with his. He held my face gently in his strong hands and caressed my cheeks with his thumbs as softly as the flutter of angel's wings. He began to cover my neck with kisses and head southward when I stopped him.

"This will go no farther! You know, of course, that I am no innocent, but this is not the time or place for your lips to proceed." I gave him a glance that I hoped would reassure him. I did not stop his lips' progress for lack of interest. Raphael must have known as well as I did that there could be no tryst beside the sea wall. That was why I'd chosen that spot. As he himself told me, "There is pleasure in the chase."

He moved away from me. "Of course, Gabriella...for now." The expression that accompanied those honeyed words was so warm and sensual that I was tempted to give in to his heart's desire, and mine. But we might be seen; and our friendship was still young. I could resist now, though just barely. The time might come when I could not.

After that dinner, our meetings were sweet but brief and rare, for summer was the busiest of times for Raphael. In the summer, all the boats needed attending. The docks, walls and buildings were in constant need of paint and repair. I saw little of him, but the looks we occasionally exchanged let me know he would have had it otherwise. I too had my duties and thanked God that when my days were busy, it served to keep my lonely nights from distressing me. I could not help but think of the curse no one was allowed to speak of. If I could discover the truth of it, perhaps, I could somehow stop these tragedies.

There was no great concert on the horizon, but still the

maestro gave me lessons. He seemed to enjoy them as much as I did. The longing I had felt for him had cooled some or been replaced with one more appropriate. The feelings we now shared were of our love of music. I felt great relief that my mortal soul was no longer in jeopardy. We rarely spoke of private matters as we once had. Music was our language. Maestro Antonio was exploring compositions for the hautboy, and as I had some skill at the instrument, I endeavored to help him with this work.

It was during one of our sessions that the maestro said to me, "Summer is the easiest season to love. You, my summer's child, are the easiest of all." A short time ago, I would have been thrilled by those same words, but thankfully my heart had changed in a more appropriate direction and Raphael filled my dreams. Still, I loved the maestro for his genius.

That summer's days were filled with hope and happiness for me. My birthday, once the focus of the summer for me, came and went without comment. I found a rhythm and a purpose to my life at the Ospedale. My lessons gave me satisfaction to share my passion for music. My errands though not so vital, gave me a chance to see the workings of our community and talk to everyone and occasionally one handsome man with deep blue eyes. I was even attempting not to tell others how to do their jobs, although sometimes, I could still not resist giving advice where none was asked for. Most just laughed and said, "Thank you, countess, for your advice."

I had not forgiven Veronica for her foolishness, but I thought of all the inhabitants of the Oespedale she might be my best source of information on the curse. So I pretended to be over my hurt and we often ate and talked together. She seemed more at ease around me, as if she no longer felt threatened by me. Either she thought me her equal, which I doubted, or she felt somehow that she had won the unspoken contest between us. I did not care which, I needed information and I preferred her company to my loneliness.

One evening, as we ate supper near the seawall, I dared to pose questions I hoped would help me learn more about the terrible fact of the premature births. Veronica was smart, and I must be cunning when delving into my friend's past. "Tell me, Veronica, have you never been in love?"

"Oh, so you think you are in love with Raphael?" Her eyes shone white-hot with such emotion as I had never seen in her. "I must warn you, Gabriella, he will tire of you. His heart is not constant, and he seeks pleasure above all else." She closed her eyes and when she opened them, the fire was extinguished and the coldness had returned. "To answer your question: yes once, when I was far too young. I thought myself in love with one of the patrons who attended our concerts. He talked me into running away with him. For my love I was rewarded only with cruelty. I am wiser now."

I took her hand. "Was he the father of the child you lost?"

She tore her hand from mine and glared at me. "Who told you of my past? We share little you and I." She stood up and turned to go but stopped to look over her shoulder. "You grieve for your loss, while I was thankful not to have given birth to the child of a monster." She turned back and fled as if being chased.

I felt some sorrow for Veronica. I knew I must be patient in my search for the truth and now proceed without her help. Some little part of me could not help wonder how many secrets hid behind those sapphire eyes.

New people came and went from our town within our little town. Two new sisters came to teach Latin and Greek. One of the older girls was asked to be a governess for a great house and left us. A new priest came to replace Father Ricardo, who was too old to say mass anymore. He could not remember the words and often wandered away from the altar, leaving all at mass to shake their heads with pity. Maestro Antonio rarely said mass. It was said he was too busy, but I heard a girl say, he often had to leave the alter to catch his breath. The new priest, Father Francesco, was a much-needed addition to our ranks.

He was young and I would have called him handsome if it was not for his eyes, which shifted constantly to survey his surroundings, like a hungry wolf I had once seen in a cage. Many of the other girls did not share my assessment and were glad to have a handsome man at the Ospedale. Their girlish tittering about Father Francesco was innocent enough, I thought.

One night as I sat staring out my window once more, awake as the rest of the world slept, I saw a shadow leave our building and head to the rectory. The figure did not come back while I watched. Someone was not where she should be. This caused me a little alarm and pity for the heart and possibly even the soul of that shadowy figure. I said a prayer for her and finally fell asleep.

It was the next day, on my way to a session with Master Antonio, I overheard a conversation I should not have. I have been told I have a light step for a tall girl, and often I surprised the maestro as I approached. This time, I heard voices and stopped just outside the door.

"You may choose not to pick the flowers God so graciously put on this earth for our enjoyment, but you will not tell me what to do. The speaker was a man whose voice I did not immediately recognize.

"You will not touch those innocents. I will write to the Bishop. You have taken holy orders! Do your vows mean nothing?" Maestro Vivaldi sounded angrier than I had ever heard him.

"When you write the Bishop, be sure to tell them how you cannot abide to say mass. Then see who is removed from the Ospedale!" With those words, the speaker left the chamber. I hid behind the door and I saw the man leaving. It was Father Francesco.

Maestro Antonio's hands shook with anger as he handed me the score for this lesson. I took my seat upon the chair in front of the hautboy and began to play the new music. He stopped me by putting a hand across the pages.

"Gabriella, I must speak to you of a grave matter. Do you have knowledge of any of our young ladies acting inappropriately toward Father Francesco?"

"The girls often giggle and make silly comments. Some find him handsome. Such things are normal for young girls. They do the same for most of the male occupants of our Ospedale."

"Even an old man like me?" he asked, though he well knew the answer.

"Especially for the genius that is our maestro," I assured him. In truth, many of the female residents of the Ospedale had thought themselves in love with our maestro at one time or another, as he knew all too well.

"You have no evidence of any…consummation?".

I remembered the shadow I had seen leaving our building, hesitated, but answered him at last. "I did see a girl leave our building very late and not return. It is not really evidence, but it did seem odd to me."

"Do you think it could have been Veronica?" Master Antonio asked.

I thought for a long moment. "I did not hear her door open. It, it was a small shadow and Veronica is certainly not tall." This was only speculation and I do not wish to sully a reputation. Wondering at his point, I was afraid to ask why he was so troubled. Why was the maestro so concerned for Veronica? Could he know anything about the curse?

"Maestro, I have heard stories of a curse at the Oespedale. That…

There is no such thing as a curse!" he bellowed at me. "I should think a girl of your intelligence would not fall for such superstition."

"I do not believe in curses, but do you not find it strange that no child has survived its birth at the Ospedale for years?"

He sat silent for a long while. "I have no knowledge of such a thing. That is not my concern right now. Father Francesco has shown an unusual and improper interest in our students," the maestro said with mounting anger. "He has few duties that include contact with our students, yet he can almost always be found surrounded by a circle of adoring young girls. While I understand that any new and novel addition will attract such attention, he has admitted to me an unholy desire toward these innocents. I will not have it!" He pounded his fist on his writing desk. "These girls are our precious charges; they were not raised up as chickens ripe for plucking."

"We are all human, Antonio. Sometimes we feel what we should not."

This brought him back to himself, as I thought it might. He understood my reference.

"I am aware of this. I also know of your growing interest in our Overseer, Raphael. I have eyes, Gabriella." He took a seat in his wooden chair as he always did to watch me play, but some thought still creased his brow. "Such appropriate feeling between two people of similar ages and stations can be wonderful, I am told. I will not allow any figure of the church's authority to use that station to prey on our girls for his unholy carnal pleasure." He paused thoughtfully for a moment. "I mention Veronica because she has not been acting herself of late. She has been skipping her lessons. I am not sure how much you know of our virtuoso violinist."

"I know she has little room in her heart and I believe something must have caused this."

"Yes, very perceptive. Veronica has had great sorrow in her past and requires special consideration. I spend more time with her than any of you because it seems to ease her suffering."

I wondered if he truly knew Veronica at all, as I knew I did not. I required more of an explanation, asked and was given it.

"She came to us as a small child. She did not speak at all, though she was old enough. Her mother had died, and some trauma had left her mute. I started her lessons much sooner than usual as a therapy. I hoped to reach behind the silence in those beautiful, sad eyes. She loved the violin and displayed a great aptitude very early.

"My treatment worked. After a year of lessons, she began speaking. It was as though nothing had happened and she seemed a normal child. Sister Maria, who was in charge of the little girls at the time, reported to me Veronica often woke in the night screaming and begging her mother to wake up. It would have broken your heart.

"The longer she was here, the less often she had nightmares. She grew calmer. Veronica loved the evening performances and often stayed after to talk to the patrons, though this is not usually allowed. There was one gentleman who grew enamored of her. She was too young to have such a desire but she had always been indulged. To the surprise of everyone, the man asked for Veronica's hand in marriage. It is forbidden for our students to marry before the age of sixteen and Veronica was only eleven at the time. She was far too young to be taken from us. We had hoped she would wait patiently or that the man's infatuation would pass."

"One night she disappeared. Everyone feared for her. After all the girls were questioned, and secrets shared were revealed, the headmistress went to the patron's house to retrieve Veronica. Sister found her beaten nearly to death and horribly abused in ways I will not discuss." The maestro walked to where I sat and put his hand on my shoulder. "The man, who was both wealthy and powerful, could not be found."

"During her difficult recovery, it was discovered to everyone's horror that Veronica was with child. She was only a child herself, having not yet turned twelve. God mercifully took that child too soon. Veronica did not acknowledge what had happened and never spoke of the loss. All she would say was, "I was sick. Now I am better, as my mother told me." No one knew what her words meant, but we were grateful she seemed unscathed by the horror of it all."

Antonio's eyes filled with tears. He blinked them away and looked at me thoughtfully.

"I have seen great coldness in Veronica," I said. "I could never imagine the source of it to be so terrible." I wanted to find her and hold her in my arms and tell her I would always be here for her. I felt a wave of nausea at what that little child must have seen and endured.

After a few moments, Antonio began again. "Our winter's girl is fragile and must not be hurt again. Sometimes she seems unbalanced and does or says things she should not. The last time we had a session, she expressed a highly improper interest in our new priest. I do not trust Father Francesco. He pays far too much attention to all the girls. I would appreciate your help protecting the girls from him."

"I'm not afraid of him," I answered resolutely. "Fortunately, he does not seem interested in me, perhaps because I see his wolf's eyes and am not fooled by a handsome shell. I will watch, Maestro, and report what I see.

"You are wise as well as lovely, Gabriella. Let us enjoy a little hautboy in D minor today to lift our spirits." Though we played for over an hour, this beautiful piece could not erase my sick feeling. The truth about Veronica hurt me almost as if it had happened to me. I was sorry to ever have argued or held back my friendship, but it was not easy to be close to Veronica. I would watch this wolf dressed in a priest's cassock.

CHAPTER SIXTEEN

The next morning, I was deep in thought as I gently reached beneath each hen to remove the egg she had laid and hoped to hatch. I held out my hand and rewarded each girl with a little corn for giving me her prize. I had taken Raphael's advice and asked Marietta how to retrieve the eggs without violence and had taken her expert advice. Tessie, the large red hen, was the most reliable layer, but she liked to peck anyone trying to steal her baby. "I understand, Tess. One day I will let you keep one, I promise." I stroked her head softly as Marietta had advised.

Suddenly, I was grabbed from behind. Without thinking, I reached into a fold in my work clothes' sleeves and came up holding my father's little dagger. Then I saw Raphael, and the shock on his face made me laugh.

"Cannot a man seek a little kiss without being gutted like some cod?" he demanded.

"My father gave me this knife for my protection when I had to leave my home. It has come in handy." I slipped it back into my sleeve. He smiled in approval, gave me a quick kiss, and headed off about his important duties. I carried sweet memories with me all my day. I could almost feel his lips on mine as I went about my daily business.

The hot summer days gave way to the cooler ones of fall, yet I saw less and less of Raphael. When I asked Veronica, she told me that he had a house on the mainland and spent time there. She seemed distracted and was hardly able to spare a moment for conversation. I decided then to take more notice of Veronica's actions.

After a few days I found a pattern. Lessons more lessons and quite often she spent time at the infirmary with sister Maria. I had never known her to care about the wellbeing of others previously, and her interest in the sick surprised me. Now each day she could be found at the infirmary tending to a girl who was sick or a boy who injured his hand. I thought this was a healthy thing for Veronica to help others, but it led me no closer to the truth of why no child could survive to be born here.

One dark night as I watched out the window, I saw a small shadow leave the building and I determined this time to follow it. I opened the door slowly and as I stepped out the door, I was stopped by something hard across my middle.

"Where are you going at this time of the night," said Sister Theresa, blocking my way with her broom. "All good girls are in their beds. See that you go back there this instant or headmistress will hear of this."

Heading back to my room, I could not help but wonder how that shadow of a girl got past sister and out of the building and exactly where she went.

Returning to my room, I knocked softly on Veronica's door. There was no reply. I knocked for long enough that she could not have slept through such racket. I hoped not to rouse the girl who lived in the room next to mine. I carefully pushed open the door to see for myself that the room was empty.

I had never been in Veronica's room, even in our early days. My chamber was larger, and she used to love to lie on my silk pillows as we shared stories. It seemed strange to see that blankets covered her windows to conceal a candle left burning. I felt compelled to go in. Her room held very little: a bed, a small cupboard for her clothes, and a table where the candle burned. Above the table on the wall was a small painting of a cherubic child who seemed to gaze down upon the room. On the ornate wooden frame were a series of marks carved into the wood. In front of the table was a little wooden prayer bench. It made me sad to see the little altar she had created to honor her lost child. On the windowsill, I saw three jars. It looked like each contained some sort of grain. I opened one to find the grain had molded. I returned to my room lest I be discovered upon her return. Her actions were odd, but I had no idea why she kept those jars when she had little else in her room. Who was the child in the picture? I raised far more questions that I had answered by snooping in Veronica's room.

I lay wondering about the significance of the things in Veronica's room. I said some silent prayers that she would soon be safely in her bed. Though we were no longer close, I did not wish ill for her. I decided to wait up until she returned to intercept and talk with her. The next thing I knew, I was awakened by the sound of her door opening and closing. I got out of bed at once and knocked on her door.

Veronica took a long time to answer. When she did come to the door, she had donned her night dress and mussed her hair to look as if she'd been sleeping. "What is it at this hour, Gabriella?" Irritation was all I could read in her face. Her breathing seemed to come hard, as if she had been running, and I thought I could smell wine on her.

"I was worried about you, Veronica. I knocked earlier, and you did not answer."

"I have been here all night. You did not knock hard enough," she said with a frosty glare.

"I know you were not in your room."

"You have no right…" She tried to close the door, but I stuck in my foot.

"Did you meet someone? I don't care what you do, but the maestro is worried. I just…

"Oh, so you are doing his bidding now? Tell Antonio that where I go and with whom I meet is none of his concern. I believe that he is jealous." Her eyes looked a little wild and unfocused.

"He is concerned for you, as am I."

"Well, you can both keep your concern. I have no use for it."

She managed to push my foot with hers out of the doorway and slammed the door.

I lay awake most of the rest of the night, wondering at Veronica's strange behavior. I must find a way to follow her next time and catch her in whatever she had been doing out in the night. The maestro had a good idea of what was causing Veronica's strange behavior. I prayed to Almighty God he was wrong.

My friendship with Veronica could never be repaired, but I was determined to remain polite and even exchanged pleasantries upon occasion. I had to remember she had been very kind to me when first I came to the Ospedale and she was Raphael's sister.

As Raphael and I shared a rare dinner on the seawall the next day, I brought up the subject of his sister's tragedy. His eyes narrowed, and I glimpsed the same coldness I often saw in Veronica's eyes. He answered with uncharacteristic harshness. "I do not wish to talk of this, now or ever. My sister has had more pain in her young life than any one woman should ever have to know." He made his excuses then, and I did not see him for days.

I stopped in at the smithy one day, eager for word of him. It struck me as I entered that there was no fire in the furnace and far less activity about the place than usual. A short and stocky boy pushed a broom as if he had all day to sweep one square foot.

"Rodrigo," I said, "That is your name, isn't it?" The boy nodded and looked at his broom.

"You need to move that broom a little faster if you want to get that floor swept by Christmas."

He glanced up with his head cocked to one side but said not a word.

"Do you know where our overseer is and perhaps when he might be expected to return?"

"Ain't none of my business, but he told me to tell you he was in Verona buying equipment and such," said the boy. He kicked the dirt in front of him but avoided my eyes. He did not return to his sweeping but stood staring at the ground.

"Do you have something else to tell me, Rodrigo,?" I asked, for it seemed that he did.

"I don't really want to say, but... I think Raphael has a girl in Verona."

"Why would you think this?"

"Our overseer don't sleep here most nights and sometimes stays gone for days. He told me to tell you he went for equipment, but I know he done no such thing. I don't think 'tis right to lie, specially to a lady like you. I would not lie to you if you was my lady." Then he busied himself with sweeping, and I walked away.

Though I'd kept my composure, Rodrigo's words hit me like a cold bucket of water, dowsing me to the bone. Why would Raphael tell anyone to lie to me?

I set out to find Veronica and discovered her in the infirmary, serving tea to a pale girl who smiled gratefully. I waited for her. Sister Maria stood at the girl's bedside and wrapped the teapot in a cloth to keep it warm when Veronica finished pouring.

When the girl drank the last of the tea, Veronica turned to leave and saw me waiting for her. "What can I do for you, Gabriella? Perhaps some violin lessons?"

I managed to laugh at her reference to the little joke that had long ago lost its humor.

"If you are not careful, Veronica, I will take you up on that offer. May I walk with you? I wish to speak to you of Raphael. I have not seen him in days and he told one of his smithy boys to lie to me."

"Well, Gabriella, it has finally happened. Raphael has grown tired of you, as he always does. I warned you. I hope your heart is not too badly broken." Though her words sounded concerned, her look was colder than the icy winter wind. I could do nothing but walk away, taking my tears with me.

Perhaps my heart was broken, but how could anyone who ever called me friend treat my pain so callously? I understood her loyalty to her brother, but I had done nothing to give her reason to treat me so. If our situations were reversed, I would have tried to soothe her pain, not increase it. I went to my room in a daze and shed many tears. I had cared for Raphael and hoped... I realized that such hope would have accomplished nothing.

What was wrong with those two? What monster was the mother to them both? Perhaps she could not teach them to love because she herself did not know how. What could a courtesan know of love when hers was for sale? My heart may have been in pieces, but I knew of love. My home had been filled with it. I gave over the night to pity for myself and regret that God had placed these two in the way of my life's progress. I was better off without Raphael and I found it hard to care with whom Veronica spent her nights.

I realized, as the new day dawned, that my feeling for Raphael had only distracted me from my mission to find a suitable husband in a patron. But this dalliance had cost me nothing but a little heartache and some wasted time. I knew I would survive. I always had until my sentence was pronounced and I was brought to these gallows.

The fall headed to winter, and the air turned much colder. I occasionally saw Raphael, and he always smiled; we even talked a little about general things. I saw he did not want hard feelings between us and so remained polite. There were no more stolen kisses nor lunches beside the seawall. I had learned to smile without it reaching my eyes.

CHAPTER SEVENTEEN

A glorious concert was scheduled for Christmas. I had a harpsichord solo and another on the recorder. With Raphael no longer clouding my mind, I set about my mission with renewed determination. I would absolutely find a suitable patron to be my husband. The practice of two solos was taking a great deal of time, and I was grateful not to have much time to myself. I had been too tired lately to investigate Veronica's nighttime activities. I cared too little about her or her brother to lose sleep over either of them.

Christmas came at last, and the concert was well attended. The orchestra was lovely, decked out in the finest we had to offer. I wore gold velvet trimmed in satin. It was a delicious confection of a dress, perhaps too much for a Christmas concert, but I reasoned that I might never have anywhere better to wear it. I had my curls piled high on my head, as befitted my new wiser and less girlish state. I even dared to paint a tiny beauty spot under my left eye. I had learned that this position denoted I was available. Sister Angelica would have ordered me to remove it or perhaps slapped it off my face, but the spot was small, the night was dark, and she was old. It was, of course, Veronica who taught me the language of beauty spots and often dared to wear one herself at such occasions. Hers tonight was lower on the cheek, as if she were married. It puzzled me until I decided it was just her way of taunting the sister's authority.

I was in the middle of my second solo when I glanced out over the sea of smiling patrons and thought I saw someone I knew and I missed a note. He sat in the front row, a young man in a tall powdered white wig. When our eyes met, he nodded in acknowledgment. It could not be, I thought. After all these months, he could not be here. And yet I was certain it was Tomaso Terra, my former betrothed. A surge of emotion caused me to miss another note. Thankfully, my sisters in the orchestra played on as if all was well. It was a trick we all used to cover for each other.

It seemed forever until the reception began. I hurried to the table to fetch my single glass of wine, eyes searching the crowd. I saw him standing across the room. It was indeed Tomaso. I would know that tall, broad physique anywhere. The ridiculous, though fashionable, powdered wig could not disguise him. His eyes lit up when he caught sight of me and he crossed the room, smiling his lovely, bright smile.

"You are as beautiful as first I saw you. You still take my breath away as you did that day in your family's home."

"Tomaso, what brings you to our little concert?"

"What do you think? It has taken me all this time to find you. At last I have. Are you happy here, Gabriella?"

"I am as happy as such a life can be. Your parents, I trust they are well?" I aimed for more civility than I felt. My own impetuous mistake to blame for my ruin. However, were it not for his mother's demands, Tomaso and I would be married now. Married, perhaps with a baby boy born just a little early. I now know that this would not have been the worst of deceptions, but perhaps the best. Our happiness would not have been dependent on whose blood was in the child's veins. Others of the Terra bloodline would have followed, I felt certain.

He reached over, taking my wine glass. Picking up the bottle, he filled it to the top with a charming look that caused sister 'Wine Guard' to simply back away. "It has been so difficult to go on without you. My life has been but a shadow of what it would have been with you as my wife." Setting the glass on the table, he took my hands, and enfolded both in his large warm ones. He dropped to his knees as he had done that day in my home's grand reception room. He seemed just as handsome and full of the joy of life as that first day. Tonight I was not sick with pregnancy and could see the glory of him even more clearly than ever and could find no words.

"Say nothing, my dear one. This is not the proper place. I had to see for myself that you were here. I will be back with permission. I will return for you, Gabriella." He bowed from the waist to me, then handed me my glass and took his leave.

"I stood with my mouth open, unsure if any of this was real. The good sister took my glass and poured half of its contents into another glass before handing it back to me.

Veronica approached with a rare look of envy on her beautiful face. "Who was that? Some wealthy patron enamored of our golden soloist? I think such a man could surely help ease any pain you feel from the loss of Raphael."

"Someone from long ago," I said; she deserved no more explanation. I turned from her without another word and walked back to my room alone. I lay awake thinking for a long time. Raphael had not come to see me perform my solos. This meaning was unmistakable: his sister had been correct. But why had Tomaso come? Could my prayers have been answered? Had Tomaso forgiven me and come here to find me so that we might still be married? Could the life I had ruined still be mine?

With no clear answer to any of my questions, I could not sleep for thinking of it all. In my turmoil, I heard Veronica's door open and footsteps in the hall. Lying awake in my bed, I decided to follow her. This time I would know for certain. The maestro deserved to know. He had entrusted me to find out, and I had to keep his trust; I had promised. Perhaps Veronica did not deserve our concern, but she deserved to be protected from a monster that was Father Francesco.

I threw on a cloak and crept quietly down the hall. As I approached the door, I could see Sister Theresa sitting in her chair with her broom across her lap. Her head was bobbing with sleep, but I could not take the chance. I knew the room nearest the door on the first floor was no longer occupied, as it had belonged to Tessa who had left to become a governess. Silently, I opened the door. My heart pounded as I forced up the window and climbed out. I landed in one of Sister Angelica's rose bushes, and it was everything I could do not to cry out. When I untangled myself from the thorns, I saw Veronica halfway across the courtyard and hurried to catch up as quietly as possible. Then I followed as close as I could without her seeing me.

She headed straight to the rectory, just as I thought. She went around to a side door. I saw the door open and Father Francesco's face lit by the candle he held. Looking around with wolf's eyes gleaming in the candlelight, he checked that she was alone. I stood in the shadows, unseen. He enfolded her in his arms and pulled her inside with his lips firmly on hers. It was clear he kept no vow of chastity.

In the morning, as soon as was decent, I sought Maestro Antonio and told him his suspicions were correct. I described all that I had seen. He listened with eyes closed, sitting upon the pianoforte bench. Drawing in a deep breath, he opened his eyes and looked past me across the room. "This must not be allowed to continue. I am not sure how best to handle it, but it cannot continue! Say nothing to Veronica. I will handle this matter myself." He turned to look at me. "Do not worry, my child. You have done the right thing for your friend. I can only thank you for your help." I could not bear to tell him that I did nothing for Veronica's sake. In truth, I wished only for his approval.

I encountered Raphael as I passed the stone cutters shed. He grabbed my hand and made to kiss me as if nothing had ever happened. I pulled away. "Do you think when you tell others to lie to me, I will wait for you and feel the same? I have seen you very little in the past few months. Do you think I do not deserve at least an explanation?"

"So you have taken our little flirtation as serious."

"Thank you for clearing up my misunderstanding." I turned to go and then thought of something else I had to say and turned back. "I did not take our friendship lightly, so when one of your smithy boys tells me you have another girl in Verona, what am I to think? Did you imagine that I would wait like a faithful hound after your own sister tells me you have finished with me?" I was by then in tears and I ran from him lest he notice. I now had a plan for my life, and it no longer included Raphael.

When I arrived at my room, I found Sister Angelica, the Headmistress, waiting for me. I wiped my eyes and endeavored to be strong. What she had to tell me would erase all other thoughts.

"Hello, Gabriella. I have come to speak to you of an important matter." Evidently it was important, as she had rarely spoken more than two words to me since first I came. "I am happy to say that you have attracted the attention of a very important patron. This man wishes to make a large donation to our school and wishes you to help him with this matter. Signore Tomaso Terra would like you to help him choose a new pianoforte for our school."

I stood with my mouth open wide enough to catch flies.

"He seems to have some prior acquaintance with you and values your opinion enough to make such a request. It is not usually permitted for our girls to leave the Ospedale. However, Senore Terra insisted that you help. If you are willing, it would mean so much to us to have such a donation." The sister stopped to catch her breath and gave me an imploring look. "I would not ask this of you if you do not feel comfortable in doing so."

My heart leapt at the chance to see Tomaso again. He was not asking for my hand in marriage yet. Perhaps some time spent together would convince him of my value as a wife.

"I will be happy to help my dear home acquire such a treasure," I said, and the sister beamed at me.

I would count the hours until I could see Tomaso the next afternoon. Do you think me fickle? Raphael had hurt my poor heart deeply with his lies and his neglect, and Tomaso Terra was very handsome. There was, of course, the itch. How long ago in that grove of oak trees had my first Antonio taught me? It seemed a lifetime.

Finishing my lessons and errands, I was careful to avoid

anyone who might require an explanation of why I could not keep from smiling. I kept my head down and my mind on my tasks, which was not easy. When finally I was alone in my room, I allowed myself to dream just a little. Dreams were a luxury I rarely allowed myself since... since forever. The loss of my home, my family and my child had taken from me my dreams as well. Tomaso Terra, my once betrothed, might help restore my ability to dream once again.

Perhaps Tomaso might forgive me. After all, much of my value as a wife was still intact, if not a very small part of my anatomy.

When I rose that morning, it was all I could do to keep from smiling once again as I went about my breakfast, prayers, and lessons. The morning dragged on, but eventually, I found myself back in my room to make ready for my afternoon choosing a pianoforte and perhaps setting my life back on the right road where it belonged. I chose a traveling outfit of fine soft wool. The burgundy color and velvet trim made it just special enough for this occasion. I longed to wear my finest gown of cream satin, but a girl does not want to appear desperate and it was only afternoon.

After a little extra time arranging my hair, I went to the Head Mistress's office at the appointed time. Tomaso was waiting, and I was rewarded for my extra effort with a long, slow look of appreciation. This was the Tomaso I had first met. Gone was the silly wig; his mahogany hair was tied back with a simple ribbon. He took my hand and, as Sister Angelica looked on, gave it a polite and somewhat chaste kiss. I say "somewhat" because Tomaso was a passionate man, not one to hold back his feelings. The look he gave me as he kissed my hand was smoldering. His dark eyes through dark lashes pierced me to my core. I could not help but feel that look in a place I will not mention.

The good sister did not leave us alone but walked along with us to the dock. Tomaso had brought his own ornate gondola with two rowers for the occasion. The large boat had a little tent erected in the middle, no doubt for privacy. When Sister Angelica saw this, she let out a cluck of disapproval. "This is a gondola fit for a courtesan, not our keyboard teacher. I have arranged for one of the Ospedale's boats to take you both. The man who rows is mute, but you will not be unescorted."

I felt a little disappointment, but perhaps it was for the best this time. I had never seen the man at the oars before. He wore a large floppy hat and long greasy gray hair hung below the hat, no doubt to cover some hideous deformity, poor soul. He appeared bent with age, and I doubted he would have the strength to row. Surprisingly, he proved more than adequate.

I could hardly hear for the rushing of blood in my ears. Tomaso gave the boatman directions to our destination, and we were off through the canals.

This was my first real view of La Serinissima since my arrival and I drank in the lovely arched buildings in colors of rust, green, pink, yellow, and cream. The boat slipped past huge domed churches and tiny carved stone bridges. Many boats of every size passed by until finally the old oarsman pulled up to a wide dock.

The piano salon was a bright yellow building with small pillars that looked like twisted ribbon across the front. I was excited to see where pianos were made and sold and thrilled to be in Tomaso's company. During the half hour that it took to reach the salon, Tomaso never let go my hand or removed his eyes from mine. "I have missed you terribly, Gabriella," he said as we got out of the gondola. "Imagine how my heart ached when I learned we were not to marry. It was my parents who insisted on the examination. Such a minor thing would not have mattered to me."

This did not ring entirely true, and for the first time, a little doubt crept into my dreams of a life with Tomaso. His words continued to be of regret and undying admiration. His manner was intimate, yet formal.

This doubt was quickly pushed aside as we entered the music salon. There were many pianos on display, and after some consideration I chose not the largest or the one with the most ornately carved upright sounding box, but the one that looked built to last. Thousands of fingers would travel those keys for many years to come, I hoped. Some haggling took place and after a while a price was agreed upon and delivery was arranged. During this process, Tomaso had played the perfect gentleman, escorting a piano instructor from the Ospedale della Pieta. He was attentive and kept his distance. I was glad of it. The Ospedale was a respected institution, and I did not wish to represent it in any other way.

As soon as we were safely in the boat and on our way, his manner changed. Tomaso leaned close, and though the day was warm for winter, I could feel the heat of his flesh through his fine velvet trousers and my wool skirt. He bent to kiss me and I thought of nothing else.

Eventually, his kisses headed down my neck to my bodice. With each kiss, his tongue caressed my flesh, causing tiny shudders in my whole being. The canals of Venice were still a public place, and I pointed out to him this fact.

"Of course," he said. "We will have some dinner and talk further of our future." The thought of this made me flush with happiness. Our future was exactly what I had hoped for.

Tomaso gave the boatman some instructions and soon he was tying the boat to a dock in front of a beautiful, soft pink house. It had four stories and four beautifully carved arches adorning a wide, winding staircase. A sumptuous portico overlooked the canal. Surrounding the portico, a wall of carved stone that appeared as a woven screen of stone lace undoubtedly provided privacy. As we came to the top of the steps, I saw a table set for dinner. A sumptuous feast awaited us. It was nearly sunset, and I was sorely hungry. It would be dark by the time we returned and far past supper so there was nothing to do but to eat the food that had been prepared and left as if by angels. This afternoon would have the most perfect ending, I thought to myself.

We ate a delicious fowl in truffle sauce and other exotic dishes I had never tasted before. Tomaso told me the vegetables were a medley of those from the New World. Evening fell and we watched the sun set on the Grande Canal.

Between bites and sips and long yearning looks, Tomaso spoke to me of his life.

"Our business has nearly doubled in the last year. My father feels soon I will be ready to take charge of the business. I have grown much in the last year, Gabriella." He seemed to be pointing out to me what a good husband he would make me.

"I too have grown," I said. "I am not the same foolish girl from a country estate." I had learned in the last year that it took more than a handsome face to make a good husband. My mind wished to spend time getting to know Tomaso better, and I was enjoying his company. My body had other ideas. If Tomaso were to kiss me again, I might not care what all of Venice thought of me.

"I bought this house for you, my love," he said. "Do you like it?"

"Oh Tomaso, it is beautiful. But do you not have an estate in Verona?"

"Yes, my dear girl. That is where my wife lives." I thought I must have heard him wrong and my mouth fell open to ask for clarity, and he continued. "The simpering virgin my parents found to replace you lives there and grows huge with child. So you see, Gabriella, I have done my duty to the Terra name and am free to love you." He rose from his chair and moved toward me, his gaze smoldering.

"To love me as what? Your mistress?" My voice must have relayed my shock. This did not dissuade him in the least. He stood in front of me and began to unfasten the ties that held the bodice of my gown. I placed my hands across by chest, but he continued as if it were a game.

"Mistress, Courtesan—Gabriella, I care not what is your title. I only want to love you." His lips moved to my breasts, which he had now uncovered, and began to plant those same kisses that had thrilled me earlier, in the boat. It was the hardest thing I had ever done, but I stood up and pushed him away.

The look on his face was arresting, a combination of disbelief and anger. "Gabriella, what did you expect from me? Did you really think that I would marry you?" And he laughed contemptuously.

That cruel laugh changed my heart. Now I could not bear the

touch of his hands, let alone those lips that just minutes ago were my fondest desire.

"Get away from me, Tomaso. I will not be your mistress. I will not be anyone's courtesan. Take me back to the Ospedale." I began to tie up the front of my gown. He grabbed the ties from me and ripped the gown open to my waist.

"Oh, I will take you home, but not until you pay for that piano. Debts must be paid, my girl. What is the cost of one evening of your favors, Gabriella? I have paid one pianoforte, though I think it a little steep for a courtesan who has spent the last year in a girl's school." I stepped back away from him but stopped when I came to the wall of the house.

"Well, the debt has been incurred and payment must be rendered." He came toward me.

I am not a small girl, but Tomaso was a large and powerful man. I slapped him and made to kick him when he grabbed me around my waist. Then he lowered me to the tiled floor of the portico with blinding speed. I reached into the folds of my sleeve and felt to my horror that my dagger was not there. He pinned me down with his knees and held my dagger up in front of my eyes.

"Looking for this? The first thing one learns when dealing with courtesans is that they are always armed. One learns to disarm. I have had much more experience than you, my girl." He was laughing at me now. I tried to hit him with my fists, but he grabbed my hands and held them tight in just one of his hands.

"I took this off you when I helped you from the boat. I will have my payment." With my own dagger in his other hand, he cut open the front of my shift, corset, and the remnants of my gown; then he pinned me beneath him, naked and powerless.

Tomaso rose off me a little and made to unfasten his britches. Just when I wiggled my leg free and planned to knee him in the groin, he gasped and clutched at a thick leather strap around his throat. The man holding that strap was choking the lust and his last breath of life out of him. Tomaso went limp and slid to the floor.

I looked up at my rescuer and gasped.

CHAPTER EIGHTEEN

The boatman removed his floppy hat, long gray wig and was revealed to be not bent or old or mute, but Raphael. He took off his coat and covered me, looking aside to spare my modesty.

"Oh Gabriella, I am so sorry I did not intervene sooner. I had to make sure this—" he indicated my naked self—"was not your will. I came not to interfere, but only to be here if you should have need of me. Sister Angelica did not trust Signore Terra and arranged this disguise. Hurry, we must leave quickly. He will come around soon enough."

"He is not dead?" I quavered.

"No. If he had gone any farther, I would have killed him. Otherwise, Tomaso Terra is not worth the killing." He managed a reassuring smile and surveyed the state of my clothes. "Perhaps I can find something inside to cover you. The gown you came in will not do." He entered the open door to the house and returned quickly with a long black cloak. Certainly it belonged to Tomaso, as it was large, long and soft, made of black velvet and lined in the finest red satin. I wrapped it around me, grateful that it covered my nakedness completely. My hero half carried half dragged me to the boat with great haste.

Raphael rowed rapidly, and as the pink house disappeared in the darkness, the full weight of my situation dawned on me. Once again, I had lost a chance at future happiness. At least this time, the loss was of my choosing. As much as I'd thought I cared for Tomaso, I would not be his mistress. Another girl might have been happy living in the beautiful pink house, sharing a man with his wife and children; not I.

I stared at the dark water and shivered. The cloak was warm, but I do not recommend being naked under even the finest cloak on a winter's evening gondola ride in Venice. I shivered as much from shock as from the cold. Raphael had rowed for nearly an hour in silence when we pulled up to a neat house with wooden window boxes decorating the shuttered windows. He tied up the boat. Disoriented by the darkness and the situation, I had no idea where we were. I was happy we were not at the Ospedale, where I would have had to cross a crowded courtyard wearing only a cloak.

Raphael helped me out of the boat carefully, gallantly making an effort to keep the cloak wrapped tightly around me as we walked. Opening the locked door with a key, he felt his way to a chair and pushed me into it. Shivering, I sat in the darkness as he found candles and lit them. He knelt before me, looking up at me not with our former flirtation, but with care and reverence. "Are you truly alright, Gabriella?"

"I am cold, naked, and I have no idea where we are. I am, however, quite certain I will live." We both laughed. He moved away to build a fire in the fireplace.

It occurred to me that I had just escaped a threat to my newfound virtue only to be faced by a similar one. Though I should have felt vulnerable, I did not. With Raphael here, I felt safe. Only now did the gravity of this evening's events finally hit me. I sobbed, long and hard, while my kind and handsome hero enfolded me in his arms and let me cry as long as I had need to do.

After a fashion, I stopped my weeping. Raphael backed away and waited for me to speak. "I am not certain of your plans for this evening, but I am hardly dressed for any occasion," I said, smiling up at him weakly. His expression changed from one of grave concern to his usual slightly amused one.

He seemed relieved that I was able to make light of the

situation. "I did not think you would want to go back to the Oespedale until you had composed yourself and the courtyard had become deserted."

I had not actually been raped but merely manhandled and stripped. I would recover, or perhaps I already had. This time it was concern for Raphael that caused me to speak. "Thank you, Raphael, for saving me from Tomaso. I am not sure he would have injured me, but I would not have enjoyed his attentions. Are you sure he will survive?"

"Quite sure. The dog still breathes. He has a neck like a bull. I do think he will be surprised and disappointed at your disappearance. I did, after all, ruin his evening's entertainment. I do not think he deserves any of your concern."

"My concern is not for him." I leaned toward where he stood. "My concern is for you. Killing a successful merchant like Tomaso, would surely end with you hanged, no matter the reason. I understand that your concern for me is only the duty of our overseer to the valued keyboard teacher, but I very much appreciate the risk you took for me."

The amusement faded from his face. "That is not why I insisted to the sister that I must come along."

"I cannot imagine why anyone would take such a risk."

"Do you not know that I came because I could not bear the thought of you with him?"

"But you said…" He stopped me by gently placing his fingers upon my lips.

I looked up at him and then, in spite of the cold, let the cloak fall to the floor. My meaning was unmistakable' still he hesitated. "Is this not what you desire, Raphael?" I used what I thought to be my most irresistible tone.

"I will not take advantage of you." His words were stern, even resolute.

"How can you refuse to warm a lady on a cold winter's eve?" I teased him, and this time there was no hesitation. Raphael's lips on mine brought immediate warmth throughout my body, more in some places than in others.

His breathing was much deeper now, and he said softly, "Is this truly what you wish, Gabriella?"

"I have never wished for anything more than to love you now, Raphael." He lowered me gently to the floor beside the fire. His kisses were as sensual as Tomaso's, but with warmth and feeling I doubt Signore Terra could ever manage. His tongue traced down my neck slowly to linger on each of my breasts in turn. Now it was I whose breath was deep and ragged. Taking his time, he traced a line of moist kisses down my body, stopping just when I wished him not to stop at all. I looked at him, his hair painted by the firelight as if it were fire itself. His eyes melted my soul. The smile he gave me promised more pleasure than I had ever imagined alone in my room.

Delivering on that smile's delicious promise, Raphael stroked me slowly with his tongue where I first discovered the seat of my desire. My words are wholly inadequate to describe the pleasure he introduced me to that night. I will, however, make an attempt. When I finally reached the crowning of his attentions, I clung to him without breath or words. He merely smiled at me again. This time, it was his eyes that were halfway closed with need.

Unfastening his britches, he let them fall. Raphael wrapped his arms around me, lifting, leaning back, kissing and guiding me until I knelt above him. I reached down, taking him in my hand. The delicious hard smoothness of him made my breaths quick again, and I longed to have him inside of me. Taking this steel encased in silk, I placed it where I most desired and he gasped. I moved slowly at first, until I could no longer control the pace. When once again the depth of my pleasure reached its peak, Raphael reached up to stop me without a word. Moving slightly, he took my hand, wrapping it around his member still so hard, smooth and wet with my pleasure. I caressed his beauty until he cried out, spilling his essence into my hand. Reaching up, he pulled me down on top of him and we lay catching our breath.

"Thank you, Raphael," I said when I could speak again. "Your kind concern for me must have lessened your pleasure."

"I assure you, Gabriella, it did not." He wrapped his arm around me and pulled the cloak up to cover us. "There are other ways to avoid a child. Ways that are both more pleasurable and more secure. I was not expecting this or I would have brought a lamb skin sheath. I am usually not so ill prepared." His rakish smile faded and a serious expression crossed his handsome face. "Veronica has told me of how your planned marriage did not happen and how much it hurt you to lose your babe too soon. I cannot stand to think you would have married that Terra pig. I do not wish to cause you anything but pleasure." Lowering his head, his tongue circled the bud of my left breast and then again he kissed me. I shuddered.

"He would now have me only as his mistress," I said softly.

"I have fallen in love before at first sight, many times. Always the love fades as I learned the true nature of the girl. I have watched you grow and learn from life at the Ospedale. That first moment I picked chicken feathers out of your hair, I was affected by your beauty. As I stood watching you play at concerts, I was impressed by your talent, but many at our school are possessed of talent. It was as I watched you take advice on collecting eggs from Marietta, and resist giving instructions on things you could not know how to do, though not your nature, I began to care for you. I began to suspect you were as beautiful inside as well. I love you and I wish to make you my wife, if you will have me."

I sat up and gently backed away a little. "Raphael, I have no words. I love you, but I fear you deserve more than a ruined pianoforte teacher who once was the daughter of a Noble house in Florence. Veronica told me your father was a king."

"Your experiences in the past did not ruin you to anyone but a fool like Tomaso Terra. This caused you pain. I wish this was not so, but pain can be the tempering that makes a vessel strong. I need nothing more from you but to return the love I feel. Who my father was, matters not. What courtesan truly knows the father of her child? A child she did not want to be born. Please, my angel, say you will be my wife." He spoke with a sincerity that nearly made me weep.

"I can deny you nothing," I said. "I will be happy to marry you if you will grant me one request."

"Anything." He kissed me again, sliding down my neck ever lower.

"I wish to know what the courtesans know. Teach me what you have learned. I wish to please you as they have pleased you. I do not wish you to feel you have given up anything to love only me."

"That will take longer than one night." He kissed my nose. "But I think you have great talent for the work of Venus." The delight at such a prospect was evident on his face. "I am sure it was Veronica that told you of my past fascination with courtesans. I have grown past them. But by all means, let us begin your lessons." Raphael trailed kisses down the whole of me until he came to rest between my legs once again. Looking up at me, he said, "This little bud of flesh, my love, is the source of great pleasure for most women." I could not help letting a little moan escape. "But for you, my love, I think it is here." He tapped me gently on my forehead. Raphael knew me to the very center of my sinful soul. This was the most important thing I learned on that winter's eve that seems so long ago.

Raphael spent hours in rich and careful instruction. At nearly dawn, as we lay exhausted from that sweet work, I said, "We must get back to the Ospedale as soon as possible. If I am to sneak in wearing only a cloak, I would appreciate the cover of a little darkness."

As he rowed us back to the Ospedale, he told me of the little house that would always be special because our love was born there. "This was my mother's house. She left all she had when she died to me, her favorite son. She used this little place for special patrons that wished to remain totally anonymous. She also had a large country home and several other properties that I spend time maintaining when away from the Ospedale."

There were still many things I did not know about the man I loved. I would have enjoyed spending a lifetime learning. Alas, you know too well that is not to be. Please friends, forgive me my tears.

My tears rain upon the wood again and I feel a hand reach up and I see that Spud has climbed upon the gallows. He softly pats my shoulder. Bess has deserted her milk pail perch, and now stands leaning toward me on the stone wall that surrounds this gallows. She looks up with tears in her eyes. "Your story has changed my heart. I so wish you could have had your Raphael. Please go on and tell us how this wrong thing be done, that you stands before us on this gallows. We can do naught but listen. But listen well we will. Samuel the hangman still does not come. This will give you time and we will listen until..."

I hear the crowd break out in a murmur of discussion. The crowd parts and a little boy with a crutch walks between the people. No one says a word as the child in rags hops up to the stone wall.

"I knows it, miss. Samuel is me Pa and he set out this mornin' and he ain't been seen. Hasn't been a hangin' here since I was born that my Pa didn't do the deed." He gives me a wide smile. His cheeks are hollow and his face, filthy.

I get off my stool and walk closer to him. "What is your name, little man?" I ask.

"I'm Samuel too, and I am eight years old tomorrow."

I lean down close to him. "We share our birthday, Samuel. Thank you for the information."

Samuel stands beaming and a large bald man several rows back, squeezes between the people and scoops the boy up setting him on his shoulders.

Marco stands behind Bess and holds back the crowd with his arms spread wide. "Get back to your place you." The bald man settles into his former position in the crowd. She won't tell again 'til you are quiet enough." The crowd falls back silent once again.

Spud hops down to take his place and with my tone a little lighter, I continue.

We returned to the Ospedale just before it was fully light, and I hurried to my room. I met Veronica in the hall. Giving me a look of scorn and a chilly smile, she continued on her way to morning prayers and breakfast. I was grateful not to have to talk to her about her brother. I knew she could not be happy for us; there was not room in her heart.

I went through the next day with my heart so light that my feet scarcely touched the ground. My lessons never went better, and as I went about my errands, I enjoyed each one. I did not tell anyone how to go about their job. Love had transformed me, at least for that day.

The little black-haired girl who'd welcomed me my first day summoned me as I washed my face and hands in my room to make ready for prayers and supper.

"Sister Angelica will see you at once," said the little girl, now a bit taller than when we first met. Dread clutched at me as I feared I would have to explain why we were not getting the pianoforte.

When I arrived, to my surprise, there in front of the school, four teamsters were hauling away a large crate just the right size to hold the piano I had chosen the afternoon before. I hurried inside. Sister stood beside the beautiful instrument with a wide smile on her round face.

"Gabriella, it has arrived, and I felt you should be the first to play it." I sat down and played a little bit of my favorite Bach. The action of the new keys was quick and beautiful, but a little tuning would be needed. I was astonished that Tomaso had not stopped its delivery, grateful if a little perplexed. The piano was here, though it had certainly not been paid for as he demanded.

When I got up from the piano, I saw a small group of girls gathered behind me. They clapped for me and rushed up to see the beautiful new piano up close. This one was not painted wood, as was my own, but made of dark wood that shone as though made of polished glass. I was about to leave to return to my errands when Sister Angelica called to me.

"Gabriella, this also came, addressed to you." She held out a beautifully wrapped box with an envelope on top. "The Ospedale is certainly in your debt as well as Signore Terra's. I do hope its cost was not too dear." The look on the good sister's face was a question wrapped in a wisp of disapproval.

"I assure you, Sister Angelica, I left Tomaso Terra with my virtue intact."

She gave a sigh of relief. "It is nearly time for vespers. You may go to your room until then. Thank you again for your efforts in this matter. This pianoforte will help generations of our girls. May God richly bless you for this gift."

I rushed back to my room. I had to know what was in the beautiful box. The letter simply said "To Gabriella" in elegant script. I opened and read it with shaking hands.

To my Gabriella

I learned last night just how much I lost when, like an idiot, I refused to marry you. I could see your beauty, but the character and strength you showed me last night confirmed the tragedy of my loss. Our children, legitimate or not, would have been magnificent. With your beauty, talent, character and perhaps a little charm and financial security from me, how could they be any less. My regrets are many. I regret that my mother convinced me to break our betrothal. I regret I was not strong enough to stand up to her. I regret my actions of last evening even more and will carry these regrets with me every day of the rest of my life without you.

Your honored servant,
   Tomaso

Opening the box, I found my dagger, its gleaming gilt handle one of a kind. In all that happened last night, I had not yet missed it. I was glad to have it back and surprised by Tomaso's gallantry. It could never be said that Tomaso did not know how to touch the heart of a woman. His behavior that evening assured me that it was my great fortune that I did not become his wife. I doubt I could ever forgive him and I cannot help but feel sorry for his next target. God help her to resist the clutches of such a masculine force of nature as Tomaso Terra.

CHAPTER NINETEEN

I performed my tasks with relish as the short winter days passed. Most evenings, when my duties or our performances ended and I would previously have gone to my room, I met Raphael. My former plans to look for a husband among the patrons were forsaken. We spent our nights in each other's arms. I had learned the trick of silently watching until our guardian sister slept to creep out the door. There were many secret places in buildings of this age, and Raphael knew them all. There was a hidden entrance to the ancient tower. Vines and brush could be moved aside to reveal a small hole in the bricks that led to the stairs in the old, deserted tower. The tower was most secluded, as the regular entrance had long been bricked up, and it became our favorite place to continue my lessons in love. I brought the cloak I had taken from Tomaso. It was large, soft and would give no clue as to its origin if found there in the tower. It felt delicious against naked skin and made the forbidding tower a welcome place for Raphael and me to share our nights.

Often after finishing the work of Venus, we lay awake talking. Raphael shared with me his plans and dreams. "So you see, my darling, once my business becomes successful we can marry and our children will have reason to look up to their father." He leaned over and kissed my head. "Senore Adorno, my childhood benefactor, is teaching me about importing. I feel fortunate that he has no sons and much to teach." I loved the light in his eyes as he talked of our future.

"Venice is the gateway to the world's imported goods. I have learned much from the buying and selling I do for the Ospedale. With my experience and the profits from the sale of my mother's property, I cannot help but to succeed. I must ask you to be patient a while longer. I think perhaps no more than a year."

"That sounds wonderful, Raphael," I yawned. "I am in no hurry to leave the Ospedale. I am needed here. What has kept you here all these years?"

"I was waiting for you, of course." He kissed my neck.

"While enjoying those who came before me."

"You now benefit from this practice, do you not?"

"Did you not care for any of them, Raphael?" I said, ignoring his silly question.

"Of course, each one of them." he said now, nuzzling my neck. "You must be glad that they broke my heart, or I would be with one of them now instead of here with you."

"I doubt they broke your heart. Veronica told me you always grew tired of them."

"Veronica knows nothing of the truth of my heart. I thought I loved once. Maria Theresa most certainly broke my poor heart. She married a rich merchant three years ago."

"She must have been an idiot to let you get away. Tell me of this heartbreak. I would like to know even all of your sorrows." I took his hand in mine and kissed his calloused palm. I had come to love his strong, masculine hands, stroking me with their gentle power.

"As I know of yours, Gabriella? I will tell you if you tell me of your sorrows. Tell me, who caused your sad trip to the Garden of Innocents? Tell me of the man who caused you so much pain."

I had not thought of Antonio in a long time or of our babe. I had pushed the pain down deep and did not desire to speak of it to anyone. But this was the man with whom I wished to spend the rest of my life. I told him of Antonio. When I finished, Raphael lay silent and held me closer. Finally, he spoke. "I know such pain. I once took a trip to the Garden of Innocents. I was with Maria Theresa and I truly thought I loved her. I was not as careful as I should have been. She became pregnant, but once the curse took the child and we saw him buried, she could not bear the sight of me."

I sat upright. "You know of the curse?"

"Of course. You know as well as anyone the power of that curse on the babes of the Ospedale. No child born here has lived for six years now."

I examined his face. "I cannot believe the God in heaven would kill unborn babes for any reason. He creates them out of love. Some human person must be responsible. Is there not a way to make a child come early? You know of courtesans. Do they not do this sinful thing on purpose? I have heard girls talking of it, and Veronica once told me there were ways to keep such accidents from happening."

"Yes, there are ways. There are powders the courtesans use. I lived with my mother until I was sixteen. I saw her use such powders." He fell silent, then, and we spoke no more that night. I lay awake and thought of nothing else for hours. I could not squash a fear that Veronica knew far too much of the curse. Just before dawn, we crept back to our separate beds.

The next day, as I gave my lessons, I resolved to learn more of this curse. I asked discreet questions as I gave my lessons and learned from a much older girl that another child had been born too soon, two days ago. Mary Alisse was eager to share the news and her small blue eyes lit up with the prospect and the telling.

"The babe was born to a novice nun soon to take her vows. The girl survived by God's mercy and still lies in the infirmary."

I had to see the girl and talk to her. Someone had to discover the truth and stop this terrible thing. I knew in my heart there was no such thing as a curse.

I rushed through my afternoon errands and sent word to Raphael that I was too busy today to share the noon meal. As soon as possible, I went to the infirmary. It was almost empty except for a very pale, very young girl and Sister Maria kneeling in prayer. I approached the girl's bedside and found she was not asleep, but lay staring at the floor.

"I know the pain you feel." I knelt beside her bed and said softly, "I, too, have suffered as you suffer now. I would like to ask you some questions if you don't mind."

She looked up at me with an oddness in her expression. There seemed to be nothing behind her eyes.

I heard the door open and Veronica stood at my side in an instant. "She cannot speak to you as she is mute and has not the brains to say one word. Why have you come to question this poor unfortunate child? Get back to your piano, this is no business of yours." There was contempt in her voice, as I had never heard from her. Somewhere, fear built deep inside of me.

"Veronica, then we must talk outside. We should let her rest." I patted the girl's hand and rose, heading through the door. Sister Maria crossed herself with her rosary and gave me a benevolent smile as Veronica followed me out the door. When we were out of hearing of the suffering girl, I said, "I heard another child had been lost and I am puzzled. I do not believe in curses."

Veronica grabbed my arm and dug her nails into my flesh. "This is the work of God. What some silly keyboard teacher wonders, matters not one whit. You will not speak of this again. If I hear that you do, I will tell the headmistress how you come in at all hours of the morning." She glared at me in triumph.

"If the sister is to know of my comings and goings, she will also learn about your nightly visits with Father Francesco at the rectory!"

Veronica slapped my face with a force surprising in one so small in stature. "You will say nothing to anyone. Do you understand me?" Her voice shook with rage.

"Yes," I said, backing away. I dared not push her further. Something was very wrong.

I headed straight to the maestro's lesson chamber. He sat at his desk, writing. I was sorry to interrupt him, but the world would have to wait a little longer for whatever he was composing. "Maestro," I said, "we must talk privately of some grave matters." He looked up and placed his quill in the ink bottle. He walked to the heavy wooden door and closed it, not without difficulty, for this door was never closed. We sat on the piano bench and he took my hand.

"Tell me, Gabriella, what has you so disturbed, and who dared to lay a hand on you!" He took my chin in his hand and examined what must have been turning to a bruise by now.

"Veronica is the answer to both those questions. I followed her a few nights ago and saw her enter the rectory and run into Father Francesco's waiting arms. I am quite sure this was not the first such meeting."

Maestro Antonio let go my hand and his voice was grave. "I was afraid this was the case. I prayed to be wrong. Obviously, God does not listen to the prayers of all priests."

"I am not sure Veronica deserves your concern. She has the look of a wild animal and hit me to keep me quiet. I am sure that if she had a weapon she would have used it on me. I merely wanted information about the curse that took my child's life."

"You say she was like a wild animal. Wounded and fearful animals are the most ferocious of all. Stay away from her, please. I will handle this."

"I must tell you that she threatened to expose me." I looked down at the floor, embarrassed to discuss such things with the maestro. "Raphael and I are in love and plan to marry. Though I know it is a sin, we often spend our nights together, and Veronica has threatened to inform the headmistress of this. I am not ashamed of my love for Raphael, but I do not want to be caught in disobedience. Someday we will both leave to be married, but for now, I value my time at the Ospedale and do not wish to be scolded and thought a poor influence on the younger girls." I raised my eyes to his, fearing disapproval but finding only kindness.

"That would certainly be no surprise to Sister Angelica. Raphael has asked her permission for you two to marry. She would have to feign disapproval, but nothing would come of Veronica's revelation. Raphael has disarmed Veronica for you. He is a bright, hard-working young man. He will prosper now that all his energy is not wasted on chasing courtesans or the sillier girls of the Ospedale. That he has chosen the best our school has to offer speaks well of his intelligence. Leave this to me. I will see that she continues to look the other way." Then he went on with an air of changing the subject. "We must speak now of the Easter concert. There is a new violinist. Her name is Anna and I have never heard the like of her. She puts even our brilliant Veronica to shame."

"Veronica will not take this replacement well. Perhaps you can keep this to yourself until the Father Francesco matter is settled. I have no need of a solo. Please give Veronica the extra time. The practice may help to soothe her now as it has before. Make it a difficult one."

"Thank you for reminding me of what I should have known. My inspiration should never come before the needs of any student. Anna is in the very early spring of her life and can certainly wait for the limelight. Go now to your young man. I hope he knows what a prize he will someday take from us. The envy I feel for him is just another step in my certain descent to hell." He laughed, but it was a hollow laugh.

CHAPTER TWENTY

Easter approached, early this year, and the usual preparations filled the Ospedale with activity. Some business took Raphael away for a week, and I missed him dearly. Keeping busy, I avoided Veronica as much as possible.

She sought me out often, perhaps to keep an eye on me. It was as if she wanted me to know she was watching. I tried not to anger her. One evening she knocked upon my door after dinner, as she had done many times when we were closer. "Gabriella, are you staying in tonight? I guess whatever laborer you spend your time with is otherwise occupied." Was it possible she did not know of my love for Raphael? I found it a little strange that he had not yet told her. He knew Veronica's strange ways much better than I did, so I thought to keep it to myself. I merely shrugged and smiled in the cold and vapid way I had learned from her. She was not dressed for bed. Wondering what she was up to, I yawned and pulled back bed covers to be rid of her.

She went to her room but had not been back there long before I heard her door open. I was certain she was off to the rectory, but when I looked out my window, I saw her shadow crossing the courtyard to the infirmary. Strange, I thought. She had not seemed ill. Throwing my cloak over my nightdress, I hurried after her.

I stood outside the dispensary shivering behind a shrub to see

Veronica through the window, pouring tea into the cup and giving the cup to someone on a cot. I found it unlikely that she would be so caring and at this hour of the evening. I had no reason to be there and did not wish to receive one of her slaps, and so hurried back to my room. Her actions made no sense, but perhaps they should have. After quite a long while lying awake and pondering her actions and their every meaning, I resolved to confront her. To risk another blow was something I had to do. My skin would heal.

In the morning, as I headed to my lessons, I noticed two things that would change the Ospedale forever. First, I saw Father Francesco and all his belongings being loaded onto a boat—not, it appeared, of his own free will. He was arguing with Maestro Vivaldi, while Sister Angelica stood by sternly, overseeing the loading. As the boat pulled away from the dock, Father Francesco called back, "You will not be rid of me so easily, Vivaldi. I have friends!"

The maestro and the headmistress exchanged a nod and a grim smile.

I watched them walk back from the dock. They were intercepted by a little girl who ran to Sister and tugged on her arm desperately. "Sister, sister, come quick to the infirmary, and you too, Father. Hurry!"

I could not resist following. Just inside the door of the infirmary, a body lay wrapped in a white sheet. Blood soaked the sheet through and pooled on the floor. Was it the girl I saw Veronica with last night? I wondered in horror. Could she know something of this? Dropping off my eggs at the kitchen, I ran to find her.

At that time of day she was usually giving lessons, but she was not in her music room. I checked the other practice rooms and found her nowhere. I ran to our dormitory to seek her there. As soon as I turned down the hall, I could hear the cries of someone screaming in agony. I knew who was screaming, and I thought I knew why. From outside Veronica's door I heard sounds like a wounded animal, punctuated with cries of…. "Why?"

I didn't know what to do. Part of me wanted to help her, part of me knew she would blame me and wanted to flee her wrath. The decision was made for me when the door flew open. Veronica grabbed my arm and pulled me roughly inside. She shut the door and stood in front of it to block my exit. I was six inches taller than her, but she had wild strength and the element of surprise on her side. Glaring at me she said, "Did you know of this? Did you know they were sending him away?"

"No Veronica, I swear to you I did not. But perhaps it is for the best." Reasoning with Veronica in this state was like arguing with the wind. Her eyes grew wide, and I readied myself for another slap, or worse.

"What do you care? Whatever pig tender or stone cutter you are currently rutting with will still be here. If not, I am sure you will find another, easily. Francesco was elegant and sophisticated, unlike whatever workman for whom you spread your legs. Tell me who it is, whore. Who do you sneak off to each night?"

I considered the pain of her past and her state of grief. She had insulted the man I loved and I could not help but confront her with the truth. "You know it is your brother, Raphael. I am in love with him and he with me. We are to be married."

I could have hit her over the head with a cooking pot and caused less shock to her cold and lovely face. "You are a whore and a liar. Raphael finished with you long ago. He goes to Verona to see which ever courtesan that strikes his fancy. He is there now." She slowly inched toward me and my heart began to pound.

"No, Veronica! He is attending to his business and making things ready for us to marry. You have been too busy with Francesco on the certain path to Hell. He is an ordained priest, for God's sake. You should be grateful for the state of your immortal soul that he is gone."

I knew as soon as the words left my mouth I should not have said them. She flew at me with the strength of twenty demons. I did not forget my childhood training. I grabbed her wrist, twisted it behind her and in an instant my sharp little dagger was at her throat.

"Be still, Veronica. He was sent away for your own good and

for the good of all the girls here. No good could come of such a liaison." She went limp in my arms. I did not fall for her trick but tightened my grip just in case. Trying to soothe her, I said. "It will be alright, Veronica. I am your friend. We all love you and will help you. You will see. Time will pass, your heart will mend and you will forget about him."

"I will never forget him. I will love him until the day I die. I am in no danger from Hell. Father Francesco absolved me each time we broke his vows." Speaking such unspeakable words seemed to calm her. I loosened my grip a little, not wanting to injure her. She seemed to relax and her tears stopped.

"Please, Gabriella, though my heart is broken, I wish to see Antonio. I need to play my violin." I let her go cautiously, and she seemed to be in control of herself again. "But first I will write a note to my brother. I am sorry not to have told him before, but I want to congratulate him and tell him I approve, and I wish both you well." She turned to look out the window. "In a way, I am glad Francesco is gone. I knew it was wrong and now I am free." She turned back to me, her face serene and rational. "I am sure, Gabriella, you are my truest friend. Was it you who told of my nightly visits to the rectory? If it was, I know you did it only to help me."

I did not trust her. However, her manner was so calm and she did seem grateful to me so I stepped back from her.

"Veronica, I only told Maestro Vivaldi to help you. I did not want you to be hurt any further." I could only hope she understood. She turned quickly to look at me. There was still a frozen smile on her lips, but some of the wildness returned to her eyes. "I will wait outside your door and go with you," I said, replacing my dagger in the folds of my sleeve. "You should not be alone, I think."

"You are too kind. I will just be a minute." Again, her words said one thing and her eyes another. I stood outside her door. This beautiful and tragically misused young woman needed God's mercy now more than ever and I prayed for it. When it seemed Veronica had long enough time alone, I knocked and opened her door. She was gone, her window wide open.

I hurried outside, but there was no sign of her. I ran to the maestro's lesson chamber. He ordered that a search for Veronica begin immediately. She was not herself, and there was no telling what she might do.

Teams of girls quit their lessons and duties to help to no avail. After two hours of searching, Veronica still had not been found. I thought to search the practice rooms once more and there, on Veronica's violin case, lay a piece of folded paper. Looking more closely, I saw my name scrawled across the paper in Veronica's own hand.

Gabriella,
    You alone are my one true friend. Please come alone and meet me in the old tower, I need you.
    Veronica

What reason could she have to send me such a note? We had not been close for months. I searched for the maestro and could find him nowhere. Raphael was away and I could not enlist his help. I looked up at the old guard tower. A small figure moved past the square window. It must be Veronica.

I did not take time to summon anyone else, though I should have. I was too afraid of what she might do to herself. I ran to the secret opening that led to the tower. We had used that opening so many times, my love and I.

Arriving at the top, I saw Veronica sitting on the edge of the stone window with her arms crossed as if she had been waiting for me. Her eyes were wild and her face as cold as the stone on which she sat.

"Thank you for coming." said Veronica. "I was counting on your compassion. It will be your undoing, you know."

"Veronica, please come down with me. Everyone is worried about you."

"Oh, I will come down, but not just yet. We need to have a little conversation. You asked me before about the curse. Do you really want to know of it, Gabriella?"

I feared her answer, but I had to know. "Yes."

"I am the curse," Veronica said.

"You must not blame yourself for something so terrible."

"Oh, but I can blame myself. I killed them all." She stood and turned back to the window. I took several small steps toward her.

"My mother told me when I was small that when babes have no father, it is best to send them back to God. I saw her do this many times." Veronica no longer sounded like a young woman of eighteen. Hers was the voice of a little child. "I saw her make the black powder from the mold that grows on rye. She told me it is best put into tea. One dose in tea, maybe two, and the child will come too early and will go back to God. I sent your babe back to God, Gabriella."

I could not move, could not breathe. I remembered the tea my new friend had given me when first I arrived, the tea she insisted I drink. Tears rolled down my cheeks.

She stared up at the wooden roof of the tower where the sky shone through. "I did it. I sent them all back to God." Her voice was still that of a child. "All the babes to be born at the Ospedale had no father to give them a name, so like my mother said, I sent them back to God. I was sorry when sometimes the mothers died, too. I think the babes held on too tight and took their mothers with them back to God. I thought that was going to happen to you, Gabriella. I was glad then that you survived to become my friend. Now I am sorry your babe's hold was not stronger. If it had taken you with it, I would still have my Francesco."

Still, I could not speak a word. To know that my child was killed on purpose by this mad creature, once my friend, was more than I could bear. I could only stand there, my eyes dry with horror and fear. I could not cry for Veronica, and even now I feel sorrow for this. She was just a little girl now, doing what her mother taught her.

She spoke again, this time in her own grown-up voice. "I know you saw the picture in my room when you sneaked in looking for me. You must have seen the picture. My mother had it commissioned, and I loved that painting of an angel babe. I kept very little when she died, but I kept that portrait. She always said it looked like me when I was little. I thought my child would have been as fair as that angel child."

She paced the room, her eyes on the floor as if gazing into the past itself. "On the frame was one mark for each child sent to sleep with the angels. The first ones were made by my mother. One is for your child, Gabriella. I should be sorry it hurt you so much." She stopped her pacing and looked up at me. "But as you said about my losing my Francesco, it was for the best." She held out her hand as if to take mine in reconciliation. Then, with lightning speed, her hand darted into the folds of my sleeve, and she grabbed my little dagger. She pointed it at me.

"See, Gabriella, I know all of your secrets. You cannot marry my brother. Not my beautiful Raphael. You are a whore who sleeps with stable hands. Our father is the king of France. I cannot let it happen." She backed away, waving the knife as if to fend me off. "You told Maestro Antonio about Francesco, and they sent my love away. You will never have Raphael. He cannot marry you if you die on the gallows." Grasping the dagger now with both hands, she drove it into her stomach while I watched, frozen in disbelief. Without a sound and white showing around her eyes like a terrified beast, she turned and stepped out the window.

CHAPTER TWENTY-ONE

It was a little while before I could bear to look out the window, through my tears, to see her broken on the stones of the seawall lying in an ever-widening dark pool of blood. Her eyes, still open, stared up at me. I stepped back and closed my eyes. When I heard screaming, I stuck my head out of the window again.

"Look, someone is up there!" shouted one of the girls gathered around Veronica. I ran back down the narrow stone stairway to the secret door. When I came out into the sunlight, a small crowd waited. The look on Sister Angelica's face was terrible indeed. In her hand was a sheet of paper. The girls backed away in fear of me.

"Gabriella, we found this in Veronica's room." She handed the paper to me. It was addressed to Raphael. It must have been the letter she asked for time to write before she went out the window of her room. She must have left it to be found.

My Dearest Brother,

I write this to plead for your help. I fear Gabriella has gone mad.

She was jealous of my secret love and I am afraid she means to do me grave harm. If anything happens to me, please know that I love you and I forgive her, for she is not in her right mind. She has

asked me to meet her in the deserted tower and I go now to plead with her. Perhaps she can be reasoned with.
   Your Loving Sister,
   Veronica

Looking up from the page, I saw in the Head Mistress's hand the little gold dagger my father had given me. He gave it to me for protection and it was the certain proof that sent me here to hang.

"Is this yours?" said Sister Angelica with a look that said she knew the answer.

"Yes, Sister. My father gave it to me for my protection. I would never use it to hurt anyone. Veronica went wild and used it on herself before she jumped from the tower." Several of the girls in the gathered crowd gasped at my words.

"Well, that is not for me to decide. The carbenieri have been sent for and will be here soon." I knew it was no use. My friend had set her trap too well and had given her life to ensure its success and my destruction.

"I need to talk to Maestro Vivaldi. I wish to make a confession," I pleaded. The sister merely shook her head and motioned for me to go to him.

Finding him in his practice room, if only he had been there before…. I ran to him. Seeing the look on my face, he took me in his arms.

I pleaded. "I did not do this, Maestro, please believe me." I quickly explained that Veronica was dead, and I was thought responsible.

"Of course you did not. I have been worried about Veronica's erratic behavior for some time now. She seemed to be losing her grip on the real world." He held me tight, patting my head as I had seen him do to the littlest students. "I had hoped getting rid of Francesco would help. I should have seen you were protected. I had no idea how far she would go. I am so sorry," said the maestro.

"What will happen to me?" I clung to him for dear life. "How can they believe I would do this?" I said into the folds of his cassock. "Veronica took my dagger and stabbed herself before she jumped from the tower. I was too shocked to move quickly enough. She told me she was responsible for the curse. She said she killed the children that would be born at the Ospedale. She gave the pregnant girls a poison in tea she served them, and it caused the babes to be born before their time. She did that to her child and mine. Anyone that could do such a thing must certainly be mad." I could not hold back the tears and sobbed openly.

His voice was soft and grave. "They will take you to the jail and the Council of Ten will investigate and rule."

"I am innocent. They cannot take me if I am innocent."

"I have saved a considerable sum from private commissions and will get you the best advocate. Please do not give up hope.

"Hope! Why should I not have hope? Will I be hanged? They do not hang the innocent...do they?"

He did not answer at once. Then he said, "I will do everything in my power to make sure Veronica's terrible sin is not compounded. I should have suspected her interest in the girls who were with child. I thought perhaps because of her own ordeal, she sought to help them and soothe their pain, but... His voice trailed off, as if he, too, was crying.

The carbeniari came into the room. There were three of them, tall men in black uniforms and grave faces. One held iron shackles. The maestro stood in front of me and spread his arms. "You will not shackle this young woman. She is innocent and will not try to escape."

"As you wish, Father. We were told to take into custody a murderess. We did not know it was just a girl."

"I am innocent, you cannot take me." They walked slowly, but nothing I could say would stop them. All hope was lost to me and I could not even look at them but took steps I could not feel. The maestro held on to me until the men took hold of my arms and pulled me from him. The men held my arms tight to keep me from running, I assumed. Where would one run when there is no hope?

I stop talking and I look out across the many people who came to watch me hang and instead stand listening to my tale. Tears run down Bess's cheeks. Little Spud sobs silently and even Marco dabs his eyes. The others are still, but I hear sniffling. They are touched by my telling, and this gives me some comfort. I must continue, for certainly my time is growing short.

I walked across the courtyard and saw it crowded with my fellow teachers, my students, and most of the residents of the Ospedale. The crowd parted as we moved through it, and I could hear some of the girls crying. I walked along, guided by my captors. Even wrapped in my own pain, I strained to see Raphael's face among the others, but just as I expected, he was not there. I could not even say goodbye.

Once again, my future was destroyed in the space of an afternoon. This time, however, my only mistake was to be a friend to a beautiful, talented and terribly damaged young woman. Perhaps if I had been a better friend, I would not stand here.

CHAPTER TWENTY-TWO

The trip by boat wound through the canals to the prison. This time, I could not savor the beauty of Venice. The ride seemed to take hours rather than minutes. When finally the men stopped rowing and I looked up, I saw a prison of large, unadorned stone and windowless. The men helped me out of the gondola and held me tight as we passed through St. Mark's square and into the ornate Doge's Palace. They led me across the beautiful and legendary Bridge of Sighs. I looked through the latticework of the bridge to see a gondola pass by. Was this the last thing of beauty I might ever see? That famous bridge led me into the most misery I could ever imagine. Looking out the carved stone grating one last time at the dark canal below, I inhaled deeply and gathered my courage.

Once past the bridge and inside the doorway, a stench of human filth, dampness, and death surrounded me like a fog. The men led me down a long hall with the deepest despair on display behind each set of iron bars. I squinted in the dim light at the creatures behind the bars that had once been human beings. One shirtless man, with a beard nearly to his waist and dark holes where eyes had once been, reached through the bars as I walked by and opened his mouth wide and I thought he meant to scream, but no sound came from his black hole of a mouth. I was led past a cell where a woman, completely naked, knelt on the floor of the cell rocking and crying loudly, "Don't let them hurt my baby." She held something small and dark in her arms as she rocked, and I prayed silently for her. Next to the woman's cell, I glimpsed a ghostly pale figure that appeared to be hanging from something. I could not tell if the figure was man, or woman. It mattered no longer, as the smell made it obvious this poor soul had been dead quite some time. From other cells came shrieks or moans, but mercifully, I could see no other occupants. Far down the long passageway, I heard terrifying cries that could only be produced by the agony of torture.

The men stopped and one man held my arm as the other one unlocked the iron door. They pushed me inside and slammed the door behind me. As I stood watching, they turned the key, and without a glance back, walked away. My cell was small, perhaps ten feet square, and with no window, it was as dark as night. The only source of light was a torch in the hallway several yards away. That was most likely a blessing. Such a place could only be worse in the bright light of day.

As my eyes adjusted to the dim light, I saw no furniture of any kind in my cell. The floor was covered several inches in straw of unimaginable filth. In places it seemed to move with the vermin that called this place home long before me. I could smell what must be the privy in one corner. I could not imagine using it but use it I would.

I used my feet to clear the straw away in a spot near the bars and sat down, hugging my knees. The stone floor, cold and unforgiving, was better than letting that filthy straw touch any part of me. I would not think of Raphael in here. It was too dark, and he was too bright. I rightly feared I would never taste my love's lips again.

It was impossible in that place to tell day from night. I had no idea how long I'd been there when I woke to someone hitting the bars with a metal cup.

"Time for your meal, girl." Those words came from a short, stout man with a nasty sneer on a pock-marked face. Looking at me with black, piggish eyes, he reached up to smooth his sparse black hair, which was so greasy and matted that not a single hair moved as he raked his hand through it. His clothes were covered in all manner of dirt. If possible, he smelled even worse than my cell. Passing me a cup through a square opening, evidently designed for this purpose, he threw a crust of black bread through the bars. I was very thirsty and drank the liquid in a single gulp. It left a greasy film on the roof of my mouth and I was not really sure it was water. My stomach, previously empty, threatened to give the liquid right back. I looked for the bread and found it already being carried off by rats. I was not that hungry yet.

I sat back down on the stones, leaning on the bars to avoid the dank and heavily inhabited back of the cell. And there I stayed, huddling against the metal. The next time the jailer threw the bread, I caught it before it reached the straw.

"Very good, girl. You might live to swing on the gallows." He scratched his armpits and with his face close to the bars, said, "Bet you're gettin hungry, aint ya? You bein' a big strappin' healthy girl. Bet you don't have the appetite of a bird like some them girls. Some them don't last but a week." He paced back and forth, looking at me with his pig's eyes. "Let Luigi know when you want more than bread. Key or no key, you could earn yourself a nice piece of cheese."

Though hunger filled my every thought, I could not bear to contemplate what I would have to do for that cheese. I thought of Maestro Vivaldi and how he found inspiration from his hunger. There was no inspiration to be found here in this circle of hell.

Strangely, the sounds from the other prisoners became like a terrible concerto of misery that I accepted as the sound of my life now and I fell asleep. I slept, and I waited. This ritual continued for perhaps two weeks, give or take a day. I could not be certain, but I guessed they fed me once a day. Splitting my waking hours between crying and praying, I did not think of Raphael when awake. When asleep, I dreamed of nothing else.

My clothes grew loose, and I lost strength each day.

Determined not to grow weaker, I added pacing to my retinue of activities. I cleared a little path in the straw and paced back and forth. But that merely increased my hunger. I began to think of ways to keep my mind from leaving me and found a piece of white stone that was soft enough to mark the dark stone of the floor. I drew a keyboard of only one octave before the stone broke into pieces too small to draw with anymore. Placing my fingers on the marks I imagined were keys, I played as many of my favorite pieces as I could remember or imagine. Sometimes it seemed the residents of this terrible place kept time with my imaginary performance with their screams, moans and shrieks. How long might it be until I stopped being the silent principal soloist and became one of the wretched chorus of the suffering?

The day came that I felt desperate enough to ask Luigi about that piece of cheese. The toothless smile that was my answer suppressed my appetite considerably.

"I knew you couldn't long resist Luigi." Laughing, he unfastened his britches. He pressed his exposed member through the opening in the grating and said, "It's about time you used that pretty mouth of yours for somethin' more than blubberin and prayin'. There ain't no God in here. Get over here, girl, and earn yourself that cheese. If I had the key, I would give you a real taste."

I came to my senses. "I would rather eat one of those rats in the corner than touch your filthy pizzle. They are cleaner, smell better and have fewer fleas." I am not sure from where that speech came, but it turned out to be a grave mistake. Luigi no longer gave me any bread and each day he presented me with his revolting manhood as if it was some glorious gift that I should cherish. In my head, growing less capable of clear thought each day, I hatched a plan.

The day came that I could take no more. I could not look at that horrible thing or its dreadful member one more time. He handed me the cup of water and undid his filthy britches as usual. I waited until he pushed the rancid thing through the bars inches from me. I moved slowly toward the bars, trying to give him a fetching look. As Luigi narrowed his eyes in anticipation, I raked the metal cup across the grating, catching his prized jewels and doing considerable damage, judging by the blood and screaming that followed. This, too, proved to be a mistake. Luigi no longer came. I did not even get water.

CHAPTER TWENTY-THREE

It did not seem long, in my weakened state, until I lay on the floor, unable to rise. It was perhaps a day or two. The rats came ever closer, I guessed, to see if I was still breathing, in certain anticipation of a hearty meal once I no longer drew breath. I gathered all my strength to open my eyes and looked into their tiny red ones to watch their whiskers twitch. Would this be the day I could no longer raise my hand to swat them away?

Just when swatting the rats seemed far too great an effort, I heard the door clang open. I was quite certain that I was dead, for above me there appeared an angel who looked exactly like Tomaso Terra. The Angel knelt down in front of me.

"Oh my dear God, Gabriella, what have they done to you?" Disregarding the filth that was now quite indistinguishable from my person, Tomaso took me in his arms and held me tight.

I said but one word, "Water."

"Certainly." And then the Angel was gone. Of course, it could not have been Tomaso. Although he had once cared for me, I doubted he had forgotten the feel of a leather strap around his throat.

I opened my eyes to see a clean silver cup filled with water held out to me. The single most delicious taste in the world is water when you have had none for days. I took a small sip, all I had strength for, and looked up at my benefactor. It was indeed Tomaso.

The door to my cell swung wide open and much activity began. An old man led in a small terrier that made short work of the rats. The privy hole was covered in fresh lime. A woman swept out the filthy straw, replacing it with fresh clean thatch, and three men carried in a large copper bathing tub. Tears filled my eyes as I watched what must certainly be a dream. Buckets of steaming water filled the tub. After a few more sips of water, I took strength in the thought of a warm bath and being clean again.

I was able to stand, and Tomaso helped me out of my filthy clothes. I felt no modesty, so reduced were my circumstances. The hot water was as close to heaven as I may ever get and cooled far too quickly. As I dried myself with the large soft cloth brought in with the tub, I looked to Tomaso to thank him, and saw tears streaming down his handsome face. I could not help but think of the last time we met and how we parted. I was grateful that he was here to help me, no matter how or why.

"I cannot thank you enough," I told him. "If I were not now a pitiful bag of bones and beyond all desiring, I might just show you how much." My feeble levity did not seem to lessen the pain in his face at all.

"Gabriella, please know that we had no idea you were being treated so poorly. I bribed the head guard to keep the key, thinking that would protect you. It has taken us a while to find someone with enough power that bribes could be useful. Raphael wasted too much time and gold on the wrong people."

"Raphael! He is here?" My heart leapt that I might see my love again. I had given up all hope of any such joy.

"No, not just now, but he will come soon. Only one of us could come in at a time, no matter the bribe. Otherwise gold can buy all the comforts one requires, even in here."

I leaned against the bars, determined to remain upright, and sipped my water, clutching the lovely soft cloth around me.

Tomaso left the cell, whose door no longer seemed to be locked, and came back carrying a trunk. He opened it and took out some clothes for me. Clean clothes, one more answer to my many prayers. He left again as I dressed and reappeared, followed by two men carrying two chairs, a table and enough candles to light this dungeon for a year.

The next trip produces a small but comfortable bed, complete with clean linen. Finally, Tomaso brought in a basket, that by the smell of it, contained food. At the scent, my mouth watered. He smiled to see my excitement but warned, "You must eat just a little at first. There will be more later."

He opened the basket and placed roast pork, bread, and cheese on the table. It was difficult to eat slowly, but I managed to control myself. He poured two glasses of wine from a bottle he took out of that beautiful basket and sat down with me at the table. I finally stopped eating and picked up my wineglass. I took one small sip for courage, then said, "Tomaso, I could not have gone on much longer. You saved my life, and as you yourself once told me, debts must be paid."

I rose from my seat and went to stand beside him. "I have only gratitude and nothing else left to pay the debt I owe you." I looked into his deep dark eyes, hoping to see a little of his previous desire for me for no other reason than to prove myself still worthy of desiring. I desperately wanted this lovely man to take me in his arms and make me feel alive again before I give up this life. I put my arms around his neck and made to kiss him. He pushed me away gently, in his eyes I saw only pity. I returned to my chair.

"I don't blame you for no longer wanting me. I am clean now but I am afraid I left much of my former beauty in this filthy and miserable place."

"You are wrong, Gabriella. This ordeal has sharpened your beauty like a gem cutter does to the most precious stone. You could use some more food to return your curves, but your beauty is very much intact."

He seemed to mean it yet did not act accordingly.

"I do not blame you for feeling only pity for me."

"You are far more precious than the price of some food and furniture, or even a pianoforte. I can never apologize enough for behaving so despicably that evening. You owe me nothing. It was Raphael that had all this brought here for you. I just paid the bribes to get it in. Get some rest and eat small amounts as often as you can. We will see about lovemaking when you are stronger."

I could tell he was teasing me, but it warmed my heart just the same.

Tomaso locked the door and told me he had the only key so I would be safe. I ate a little and then fell asleep in what seemed the most comfortable bed in the world. The sleep was deep and dreamless.

I could have been asleep for a week for all I could tell, but when I woke, I felt very much as if I would recover. Recover for what I did not yet know. The gallows, I assumed correctly.

Somehow as I slept so deeply, someone had brought fresh water to wash in and a small looking glass. I washed my face and made to arrange my hair as best I could. Perhaps Raphael would come today. That thought alone brought color to my cheeks. I was thinner, but Tomaso was right. The effect was not unpleasant. It appeared my useful beauty was indeed mostly intact. My mind was much clearer now. Had I actually offered myself to Tomaso? God forgive me.

I ate every remaining bite of food and was pacing for exercise when the door opened. Tomaso must have noticed the disappointment on my face, for he said, "Patience, my girl, he will come tomorrow. I have brought you some more food, this time some rich cakes to help you fill out that gown." I fell upon the food and ate ravenously while Tomaso watched with mild amusement. When I could eat no more, he poured us both some wine.

"It surprises me that I feel very much like myself again. Tell me, Tomaso, how is your wife? Has she delivered that child of yours yet?"

"She has given me a son." He sighed deeply. "The child resembles her people, thin and pale, and will, I fear, be as dull as his mother. At least the Terra name will go on." He finished his wine and poured himself another glass.

"And have you taken a new mistress to replace the one that got away?"

"Oh yes, I have two new mistresses. You know me to be a man of passionate appetites. It took two women to fill the hole you left in my heart. I am sure they are missing me. Neither measures up to you, but a man cannot sleep alone." This time we laughed together.

"Just say the word, Gabriella, and I will get rid of the plainer of the two and throw the other one out of the pink house I bought for you."

"I doubt either is plain," I said, laughing. I could not help but turn to a serious matter. Pretending that it would not happen cheered me, but did not change the situation.

"Do you think there is any hope I will not hang?"

He set down his wineglass and I could see in his eyes sadness and concern. "We are doing all we can." He reached over, taking my hand tenderly. "There is some hope that the Doge and the Council can be reasoned with. They will not listen to testimony from witnesses. They merely examine evidence and make decisions as if they were the Lord on High. Unfortunately, as you know, there is evidence of a damning nature. I wish I had thrown that dagger into the canal. I assure you we are doing all that is within our power."

"Who is this 'we' you speak of Tomaso?"

"Well, Raphael, of course, and the priest Vivaldi has taken a leave from the Ospedale and is doing much to help. He has connections that have been helpful and some access to funds. Did you know he is related to a Cardinal? We are a strange band: Gabriella's soldiers bound together only by our love for you. We will not rest until we get you free of this ridiculous charge."

Leaning back and pouring himself another glass of wine, he said, "To tell you the truth, I have never had much association with priests or overseers, but I find their company surprisingly agreeable. Both are quite as determined as I to help you." He planted a kiss on my hand.

"Is there really any hope that I will not hang for the crime I did not commit?"

"I assure you, if there is a way, we will find it. Do not worry. Worry makes a woman old before her time."

"I am so glad to have widened your narrow circle of friends due to my unfortunate predicament. I will rest assured that I am in good hands." Teasing Tomaso, while not a worthy pastime to occupy my last days, took my thoughts to a happier place than I now find myself. He was charming company and helped me remember the joy of my young life, too soon to be extinguished. But it was Raphael for whom my heart hungered.

We talked a while longer and as I began to yawn, he excused himself.

The next time I opened my eyes to the clanking of the iron door, it was Raphael who entered my cell. He ran into my arms, covered my face with kisses, then backed away to assess my condition a bit.

"Tomaso said you were even more beautiful, although too thin. I can see for myself that it is true. So much of what he says is only to taunt me. He was right, my love. You are more beautiful than ever." Raphael held me close and whispered against my ear. "Tomaso is jealous of our love. I know not why. He has a wife, two mistresses and still he spends endless sums on the attention of courtesans. Nothing is ever enough for him. But I am glad I did not kill him in protecting you. He has many useful acquaintances and in truth, I find by some miracle, I enjoy his company. I beg you, never tell him this." I could do nothing but look at him and thank God for him.

"Forgive me, Gabriella, I prattle on when it is your wellbeing that means the world to me." My Raphael looked as handsome as ever. I wanted nothing more than to make love to him right there on that small bed, but I was hungry and thirsty still. I would eat first.

We shared the sumptuous meal he brought. He told me of their struggle, my would-be saviors. He told me it took some time to find out where exactly I was held and who to bribe to get the most for their money. They thought I was being well fed, as they paid every day. A guard told them I was being well taken care of by a trusted man named Luigi.

"This Luigi it turned out, was nearly castrated by some prisoner and was not able to see to your needs, we were informed." The love in his earnest eyes kept me from telling him the truth. Sharing this bit of nastiness with him would change nothing. I could not let him share my pain any more than his face told me he already had. I took care of Luigi. God help me, but I am still proud of this fact. Knowing it is a sin and being proud of it compounds my sin.

I said nothing about the jailor, only thanked Raphael for the great effort they were putting forth. If the lord God would let me escape my fate, it would be these three unlikely angels who would arrange it.

After we finished the food, I wanted only one dessert, Raphael, my beloved. My eyes must have conveyed that thought clearly as he rose from his chair, picked me up in his arms, and carried me to the bed. So honest and fervent was Raphael's worship of my body that he nearly erased all memory of the last weeks of horror and suffering. His strong, rough hands caressed my every curve. His warm lips explored and adored every part of me. His tongue lingering on the places he well knew brought me greatest pleasure. When he had pleased me so well, he gently entered me. I clung to him with renewed passion I never expected to experience again. The vocal crescendo of our mutual passion rivaled the screams from those tortured by the iron maiden, if not in quality at least in volume.

We dressed quickly as guards often passed on some errand of anguish or another. We could not lie for hours in each other's arms, a luxury I feared I would never have again. We did sit holding each other close and talking in the same intimate way we once had in the tower a seeming lifetime ago. As much as I knew he loved me, there was something that I had to say.

"Raphael, you know I did not kill Veronica. She stabbed herself with my dagger and jumped before I could stop her."

"Of course, I know you could not have hurt her. I also know that Veronica was terribly disturbed. Her mind has always been fragile." Raphael looked at me with love and began to explain.

"Our mother was stunning, as you have seen, for Veronica

was her mirror image. This kind of beauty can be a curse, I think. It was to both of them. Mother felt she had no value except for her physical beauty. Her value was only the price her company would bring from wealthy men.

"That must have been a sad life for her."

"I suppose so, but she knew nothing else. She was once a kitchen maid in the great house of a courtesan as her parents had died when she was small and she was claimed by an aunt who worked in this rich house. One of the courtesan's patrons saw her as she served one day and took a fancy to her. Her career as a courtesan began at the age of twelve. She was taught the ways of her profession, but never learned to read or write."

"I cannot imagine what my life would be without reading. I never realized how fortunate I have been for my education alone."

"Yes, and I am grateful for your education. That is perhaps part of the reason I want you for my wife. Courtesans often fail at conversation and I have not met a single one that would be a suitable partner in life as you once told me your parents are." He kissed my cheek. "My mother soon grew to replace her former teacher and became quite popular among the most wealthy noblemen of Venice. She often entertained visiting princes, as her beauty had no equal. Such men are usually not given to restraint, and so the three of us were the result of such nights of royal entertainment. It cannot truly be known, but this is what my mother told me. She said Louis the XV of France was our father, though she could hardly have been sure. Certainly, the king never acknowledged us."

"I am sorry you did not know your father. I have gained such strength for mine. I am sure yours must have been very handsome. I can certainly believe you are the son of a king." I kissed his workman's hand now interlaced with mine.

"Perhaps that is why she kept us with her as long as she did, in such vain hope. Kings sometimes recognize such natural children." With his arms around me and my head on his chest, I took in his words as if they were more delicious food.

"I grew up in that great house denied nothing of material possessions. Left to fend for myself when it came to education, I knew of the pleasures of the flesh before I could read or even partake of such pleasures. Being a curious child, I often talked to mother's patrons while she bathed and made ready. One gentleman took a special interest in me, as I have told you before. I was grateful for this attention, as I longed for male companionship as any boy does. Boys need fathers."

"And girls too." I said.

"Yes, and girls too. This man who took an interest in me, Senore Adorno, was a great merchant and generous to the little fatherless boy." He stroked my head as he continued." He arranged for a tutor to teach me reading, numbers, and such. I would sit for hours listening as he told me of the wondrous things from all the world that he bought and sold. My mother even became a little jealous of this relationship, but as long as he brought her expensive gifts, she did not complain.

This education went on for four years until I was ten. Then, as had always happened with mother's patrons, Senore Adorno came no more."

"Why? What happened to him?" I asked.

"Mother's beauty always wore thin. She had little talent for conversation. The tutor, however, still came, having been paid in advance. I enjoyed my lessons until I was fourteen, when I began my own education of another kind." He looked at me with mischief now in those sapphire eyes. "I had always known of carnal pleasure as I often peeked through carelessly open doors. My mother made little effort to hide anything from me. I began to practice what I saw on our kitchen and chamber maids for my own lessons in the sensual arts."

"I can understand how those girls could find it impossible to resist you, even at such a tender age." I chimed in.

"It was about this time that Veronica was born. She was the most beautiful child anyone had ever seen. I knew I had a brother, Anton, but I was small when he was born and I remember little of him. He also was a beautiful child, my mother told me. I am certain the jealousy between brothers lessened my regret when he was sent away. Somehow, I felt only love and protection toward Veronica from the day I first held her wrapped in swaddling in my arms."

"I am certain she knew you loved her. But no love could have saved her."

"That may be my greatest regret. As I must confess when I tell you more. I have said before, Veronica grew into the image of my mother and inevitably, problems arose. Some patrons began to pay inappropriate attention to the exquisite child. I tried to encourage mother to send her to a convent school for her own protection. She could not see the wisdom of my plan. She considered Veronica as a business asset. I should have insisted and taken her myself… but I did not." There were tears in my love's eyes as he continued.

"In my mother's defense, I believe she was already ill. The French Pox often affects the mind. By the time my sister was five, Mother was at the very least using her as bait to attract unsavory patrons she would never have dealt with before her illness. When I was around, I tried to protect my little sister. But, having tired of all the girls of the house, I was constantly abroad in search of new conquests to add to my education."

I felt I had to interrupt. "Are you certain, that you could be happy with only me to love?" The look in his eyes and the kiss that followed convinced me he would have been happy to try, given that unlikely opportunity.

"Our mother died when I was away whoring. When she died, the servant girls ran off, taking everything they could carry. Veronica was left alone with our mother's body for three days. She was six years old. Afterward, she did not speak a single word for over a year. I blamed myself. I could not let her down again.

"Oh, dear merciful God. I cannot bear to think of the agony that child suffered. But you were just a child yourself."

"I was old enough to make arrangements for Veronica to come to the Ospedale. I should never have left her with my mother so ill. I will never forgive myself for that."

"You were not responsible."

"I was all she had, and I was not enough. I sought to work at any job to be had at the Ospedale, just to be near and protect her.

Once I was there, to my great delight and perhaps my detriment, I discovered the unlimited supply of my previous favorite vice, pretty girls." He stopped to give me a kiss and one of his looks full of amusement, then continued.

"I had originally intended to stay only long enough to make sure she was well taken care of. But I worked hard and learned many things, and I saw a life for me there. I won the overseer's job when the old one died, and I felt confident that I was learning skills to make a life for myself. And I needed to stay, because each time it seemed Veronica would be alright, something would happen and she would come unhinged. The only thing that ever seemed to help was her violin and Maestro Vivaldi's lessons."

"She was as talented as she was lovely," I said. "I often envied her for it, and that envy led me to feel jealous and not be the friend I should have been to her. But I began to fear something was not right with her. Her eyes were always so cold."

"You are perceptive, my love. This matter of Father Francesco must have been the final blow. Usually she confided in me. This time, I had no idea. If I had only known sooner."

My cheeks burned with shame for not telling him. My own selfish concerns took too much of my attention. I should have cared more for my friend.

"I have made many mistakes, as I have told you. The shadows grow long and the time must be short. Grant me your kind attention just a little longer. My courage is failing me as the time of my...death draws near."

Bess stands. "We will make sure you finish. If it were up to us, no innocent would hang this day." A cheer rang out from the crowd.

"Still there is no sign of Samuel. Please tell on."

Her words touch me. The entire crowd nods and shouts words of encouragement. I know there is really nothing that can be done now, no matter the good will of my friends or this kind crowd.

The prison became an unlikely retreat for me. Raphael and

Tomaso had made it comfortable, and each day I was provided with handsome and stimulating company. Tomaso came each morning and brought me food and kept me witty company for hours. I would rest awhile and Raphael would come in the evening, bringing me more food and nourishment of another kind. He often spent the night, even though the bed was small. In a few weeks, or perhaps a month, I was stronger and my clothes no longer hung as if on a nail.

Over the past few weeks, Tomaso had grown a neat, well-trimmed mustache and beard. He made this change he told me, to give himself some air of maturity as he prepared to take over his father's business. The effect made him more dashing. As the evenings passed and Raphael did not return, I began to dream of what it would be like to kiss Tomaso again.

You know me to be a great sinner and I will not pretend to be anything else in these my last minutes. I could not help longing to stroke that new beard and feel it against my thighs. I know you must think me truly wanton, but what else is there to do when alone with a handsome man in a prison cell? A handsome man who continually compliments you, and constantly reminds what you are missing.

"Gabriella, our dinner is finished, and it is time for dessert," Tomaso said one afternoon, with his chocolate brown eyes focused on my own. "Why not let me taste just one of those luscious breasts that until now I have only seen? I will leave the other one for your overseer." He slid his chair closer to me. "I know you miss Raphael, but he is not here. Why must we suffer? I am sure Raphael is an adequate lover." He was now on his feet, kissing the back of my neck. "We have known some of the same courtesans in the past, Raphael and me. While he has practiced the art of love, I have taught experienced courtesans things they could never have known without me. Believe me, Gabriella, when I tell you, nature has blessed me much more generously than Raphael. Do you not owe it to yourself at least to taste the finest wine before you settle on an inferior vintage?"

This ridiculously arrogant speech was tempered by an almost

irresistible look that combined longing with teasing. But resist, I did. I stood and moved away.

He always brought two bottles of excellent wine and I resolved not to fall into his trap. Wine could cause a girl to do things she would later regret, as we all know well. Two glasses were all I allowed myself until he left. Then I downed another glass or two in the hopes of a good night's sleep. This plan had worked before since Raphael had been away. Often I would lay awake thinking of him and even sometimes, Tomaso would enter my sinful head. God, lead me not unto temptation but deliver me from evil. If it is not too late, I prayed.

I did love Raphael, and even though he might never know, I could not betray him. My impetuous act one rainy afternoon cost me and perhaps even Tomaso a great deal of happiness. Whenever I thought of marrying Tomaso, I remember with sorrow that somewhere, on a rich estate in Verona, a girl held a child in her arms and wondered where her husband was. That girl could have been me. I don't believe any one woman would ever be enough for Tomaso Terra.

CHAPTER TWENTY-FOUR

Each morning I spent time on my knees thanking God for the gifts I had received, and I begged Him to spare my life. While on my knees one morning, I heard the door open to see none other than Maestro Antonio Vivaldi, dressed in the clothes of a noble gentleman. The effect was arresting. The priest's cassock never did him justice. The night blue velvet coat and breeches transformed him. The muscles of his legs, clearly visible in white dress stockings, drew my eyes. His auburn hair, grown long, was tied back with a black silk ribbon. He wore an expression near as dark as that ribbon. I was happy for his visit and unnerved by that grim look.

I stood as he approached and he dropped to his knees. Wrapping his arms around me, he buried his face in the folds of my skirt. The sound of his anguish rent my heart in two. "Gabriella, we have failed. The Doge has ruled. You are to hang tomorrow." He was sobbing, this man whom I respected above all others. It hurt, at that moment, even more than the terrible news he'd brought. I reached down and took his face in my hands.

"Maestro, you have done all you could. Please know how grateful I am for your help."

I had never seen such sadness in his eyes. The joy we usually shared as we played his music was gone. Even when Veronica took her own life, The maestro was strong and resigned to the horror of the situation.

"I am so sorry, Gabriella. I was so sure we spent enough gold on bribes this could not happen. This Doge is a despot and does not keep his word for any amount of gold. We did manage to get the location of your... your...

"Hanging, Maestro?" I said.

Tears still welled in his eyes.

"I can do nothing else. I do not know what it feels like to die. I do not even know what to fear. I have spent too many days in here in terror and grief for myself. It is all used up. I cannot cry or be afraid for one more wasted breath. Please tell me how you are. Are you not writing anything?" I asked, as cheerfully as possible.

"I cannot create while one of my greatest sources of inspiration suffers," he said, but then added, "I have been thinking of an opera, someday, perhaps." He got the dreamy look I always thought meant he was creating great beauty out of notes in his head.

The subject of so many operas is a tragedy. Perhaps my short life and sad story might offer this great genius inspiration. I took some small comfort from this thought.

"Please Antonio, with so little time left, can we not talk of anything else? Do you not miss the Ospedale? I am sure that all are missing you." This remark brought back the light to his eyes.

"Sister Angelica has sent a letter to that effect. I will return soon enough." The maestro smiled. "I nearly forgot," he said and reached into his coat to fetch a small recorder. He placed it in my hands as if it was a sacred object. Of all the comforts given me in this prison, Maestro Antonio alone thought to bring me something that would feed my soul.

"I would have brought a harpsichord if it were allowed, but this will have to do."

I offered him a glass of wine and endeavored to play my favorite of his concerti that I had committed to memory. I'm sure I missed a note or two, but he sat with his eyes closed drinking in the sound. I played another simple tune and in the cells around me, all fell silent. No one moaned or screamed. While I doubted their reasons for making those sounds had changed, still there was peace.

"I had thought to compose a violin work from that melody. What do you think?" I agreed it would be beautiful, though I doubted I would ever have the skill or time to play it. We talked only of music as the chorus of suffering resumed around us.

I poured him a second glass of wine and smiled just to listen to his thoughts on my greatest passion. I was so glad to see his usual lightheartedness restored a bit. Finally, we came to discuss things of a more of corporeal world.

"You, dear girl, have chosen your love well. I have watched Raphael as he handled the operations of the Ospedale surprisingly well for one so young. He continues to astonish me with his talent and ingenuity. It is quite amusing to see Tomaso and Raphael work together to a common end. Their only concern is for you, but they squabble and compete constantly. I think it brings out the best in both of them."

He laughed, his fair cheeks were now warmed by the wine. "Yes, I perceived by Raphael's face that pleasantries were indeed exchanged on his visits. Tomaso is out all night and returns smelling of courtesan's perfume and still in a foul mood. It is Raphael who starts each morn with a smile on his face."

"Yes, Maestro, I have certainly chosen well."

"Can you not call me by the name my mother gave me? I am not a priest of my own will. I have no calling, no true vocation. Have you never noticed how I cannot get through mass without my breath failing me? I cannot stand in the presence of God, holding the body and blood of his son and feel nothing but the wish that it be over. My father was a poor musician and could not afford an education for me. There was no place to turn but to the church."

He reached up to stroke my cheek. "I did not choose the priesthood. But in the end, a man is only as good as his word. I have given my word to God."

The darkest cloud came across his face. He stood and looked through the bars. "We must talk of unpleasant things, my child. I have some family connections. There is a special place at a convent in Verona where members of the clergy are executed. Such things do happen. Some people receive special treatment even when guilty of a terrible crime. It has advantages over more public places. Because you taught at the Oespedale, I used my influence to secure this place. You will be taken there tomorrow. For the world to lose one such as you is a tragedy beyond measure. Our time is growing short. Your two other soldiers have gone on to Verona and I am left here to prepare you."

"Though I have no calling, I was allowed to come to you because I would hear your confession. It is time now." He took my hands, we knelt and I closed my eyes.

"Bless me Father for I have sinned," I began. "It has been weeks since my last confession. This will be my last so I will not include the usual small matters. In my life, I have cared far too much for my own concerns. I have been given over to carnal lust far too often, and I have prayed far too little. Please grant me your mercy and forgiveness, for my greatest sin is that I have not seen so many of my actions as sins when most certainly they were. But you know, Lord God, that I am innocent of the murder of Veronica. In the name of the Father, the Son and the Holy Ghost, I ask forgiveness."

I opened my eyes to see tears streaming down the maestro's cheeks. Sadness would not be the last thing between us. As you know me to be a bold and lustful creature, I leaned over and kissed him square on his lips. He returned my kiss. It was too brief, but warm and fervent. This would have to stay with me to the end of my days, which is sadly now.

"Goodbye, Antonio," I said.

Before he closed the door to my cell, he turned back to me. "What is one more pebble in my long and certain road to hell? Thank you, Gabriella. I may see you tomorrow, though you should pretend not to know me." These puzzling words were the last thing he said to me. Maestro Vivaldi left me alone with a slam of the heavy door and a turn of the key.

I stayed on my knees and prayed a little while longer, as you would expect of someone on the last night of her life. I asked almighty God, ever merciful, if he could not save me to please take care of my three earth-bound angels. I asked him to please help the maestro to go back to his music with the joy for life that could always be found in the works he composed. Please help Tomaso to be satisfied with the richness of his life and not continually search for more. Lastly, I asked for God to help Raphael to find love again in someone worthy of him. I downed the last of the wine and, remarkably, fell to sleep.

> *I stopped to catch my breath for just a moment.*
> *The look on Marco's face was now grave. "I had heard a fellow say that a new hangman had been spotted and was on his way."*
> *The little man now reaches in his pack and brings out a bundle wrapped in velvet. Carefully unwrapping the treasure, he reveals a small violin, like those we use to teach the smaller children. He produces a little bow from his pack and begins to play one of the loveliest of my maestro's many lively pieces. When he is finished, he bows to the crowd, which again lets out a raucous cheer. He looks up at me. I wonder at how much more there is to this little man that I will never get to know.*
> *"Thank you Spud. That was lovely."*
> *I begin again.*

The jarring noise of the cell's door brought me quickly out of a dream and to the waking terror of this day. My eyes snapped open, and it felt as if a fist of iron closed around my stomach. Before me stood two of the Doge's men in red velvet livery and silver helmets, complete with white ostrich feathers. My hanging evidently was a formal occasion.

One of the men held shackles and this time there was no one here to demand they not be used. I stood up and putting my hands behind me, gave the men a bright and wholly inappropriate smile. This took them by surprise, as I intended. This was my final performance. I could control nothing but my emotions, and I would use those for maximum effect. These men would not rest easy tonight. I said nothing and walked out of the horror of this place into the sunlight of this beautiful day. I said a little prayer of thanks to God for the beauty of this day. The sky was cloudless and the summer air soft and fair just after dawn. I asked one of my guards the date and was told it was the eleventh of June, the day before my nineteenth birthday.

The sun on my face after so long in the darkness felt glorious. It did not make me forget my plight, but it made it easier to continue my performance. I would be brave and smile to my last breath. The boat that morning was comfortable except for the shackles around my wrists. I was determined to ignore the pain in my shoulders and the iron cutting into my skin. I drank in the sight of La Serenisima with her beautiful buildings in all their softly colored glory as we were rowed down the canals. Once again, I was sorry I had never gotten to explore among them. One of my captors turned to check on me periodically. My apparent happiness disturbed. I could not resist speaking to him. "I know it is not your fault that I will hang today, even though I am innocent," I said, smiling. The expression on his face went from serious to grim. I know it was perverse of me, but I enjoyed this little torture just the same.

We arrived at the shore and one of the guards picked me up, holding me as close as a lover. I think they feared that, being insane, I might jump overboard and drown myself. This made me chuckle softly, thus reinforcing this opinion. There on the shore stood my final transportation, a luxurious carriage. Because there was a lock on the door to the carriage, I was relieved of my shackles and I thanked both of the guards for it. The looks that passed between them were increasingly uncomfortable as they sat on either side of me. Exactly my intention: hanging the innocent should not be easy.

The trip by carriage took over an hour, and I spent the time pretending to enjoy the sights, maintaining my air of false calm. Strangely, the longer I pretended, the less false this calm became. Finally, as we came to a stop, I could no longer maintain my smile. I was, however, determined to hold my head high and not abandon my dignity. I am Maria Gabriella Constanzi Pompeii, as I have said, and I will act accordingly to my last breath. A neat wooden sign on the Gate to the Convent read, "Convent of The Immaculata."

They lead me in between two large stone buildings surrounded by tall trees. Living in Venice for these past months, I had sorely missed the tall trees. Leading me to a door and into a small room, they stand as far from me as possible just inside the door. A bent old nun, all in black with skin the color of a nut and hair with no color at all, stood waiting for me. The guards look like stone statues in red. I tried to make eye contact, but to no avail. They were both quite young, I noticed, neither much older than I, and I felt a little sorry for my spitefulness, but just a little. The ancient nun gave me a severe look and motioned to a chair where a white muslin garment is draped. I assumed that I am to put this on. The old lady says not a word. I turn my back to the soldiers, strip off my gown and don this white garment without shame.

Just when I had come to expect silence, assuming the nun was mute, she spoke. "You must be someone special. This gallows is not for common folk. The luxury it affords the condemned is more than most deserve. A cardinal himself came to make the arrangements for you." She comes close and squints to examine me. "A rare sight indeed, here. We never see people of such stature here, unless they are to be hanged." She laughs. It is a toothless, raspy laugh like the rustling of fall leaves, and it chills me.

"I assure you I am no one," I said quietly. I wanted to ask exactly what luxury I was to be afforded, but I could not bear another sound of any kind from that living gargoyle.

Again, she spat dry words at me. "This gallows is surrounded by a wall and the hanged does their dance of death in private. A luxury few deserve."

At last, the mystery was solved, though the answer comforted me not. The soldiers approached and took me by each arm. They led me out the door toward a structure I recognize as the gallows. My knees began to shake. They buckled, and I nearly stumbled going up the stairs, but the guards held me tight and I did not miss a step.

Now I look up at the tall trees that have kept the sun off of me these long hours. I see the wall surrounding this gallows so that my final gasps will not be witnessed. I hope you will not begrudge me this one dignity, I beg you not to pity me but to smile when you think of me. I beg you to send your prayers to heaven for my soul.

From the gathered crowd, I hear sobs and wailing. Bess is on her knees. Many in the crowd raise folded hands in to the air and there are tears upon their faces. From the corner of my eye, I catch a flash of red, and I turn to see a line of soldiers approaching. My time has come.

I hear a murmur that the hangman has arrived. A man mounts the steps and walks toward me. The wind picks up and whips his curly black hair, obscuring his face. He carries a leather bag. I watch as he removes gloves from the bag and slowly dons them. He then takes a rope from the bag and walks toward me.

The crowd is silent. It is if there is no one but my hangman and I anywhere around. We stand alone on this gallows. He helps me to my feet and I walk toward the wooden support from which the rope will hang. I stand still as he fixes the rope to the support and then walks in front of me. As he lifts the rope to place it around my neck, the wind blows the dark curls from his face and he gives me a sly smile. I think I know that face, but when the dark curls again obscure his face, yet I know I must be wrong. He leans toward me to place the rope around my neck and whispers, "Do everything you are told."

He tightens the rope. "Kneel," says the hangman. I obey.

Someone stands beside me whispering prayers in Latin. He traces the sign of the cross on my head with sweet-smelling oil. In my misery, I realize too late that it is Maestro Vivaldi, but he is gone in a flash of white robes and red hair.

The crowd grows restless and shouts of, "mercy," ring out. As I look up, twenty soldiers form a line in front of the gallows.

I hear Bess cry, "Give her mercy, the child is innocent."

"You can't hang an innocent girl," yells someone in the crowd. A strange voice behind me booms out at the crowd.

"On this day 11th of June in the year 1718, The Doge of

Venice and the Council of Ten order the execution of one Maria Gabriella Constanzi Pompeii for the murder of Veronica Angelina Natalia Mastrianno. The court has so ruled and the sentence is now to be carried out." The hangman pulls a hood over my head. It is thick and I can see nothing.

Amid shouting and the sounds of scuffling, I hear someone order the people to fall back. I hear screams and the boards fall out from beneath me.

CHAPTER TWENTY-FIVE

I drop, but instead of feeling the rope choke the life from me, I feel ground beneath my feet.

"Silence!" whispers someone behind me, and the rope is pulled violently back and forth. It cuts the flesh of my neck, but I am silent as instructed. I hear the crowd gasp as the person behind me stops the jerking motion and pulls the rope back and forth as if it were swinging with the weight of a body. The movements are smaller and smaller until it stops. My hood is pulled off and the whispering voice behind me says. "Be still, my love. We must make a good show."

My heart leaps and I turn to see Raphael with his fingers to his lips. "You must be silent if you are to live." He pulls the rope, still around my neck, hard cutting into the flesh of my throat. I make no sound. I feel him rub something sticky on the wounds.

"Berry juice," he says, and the door to the stone enclosure opens. I see the hangman silhouetted against the bright outside light. He is smirking, and I recognize him. Antonio, our former stable boy, and my former obsession. He puts his fingers to his lips and closes the door. He bends down and whispers in my ear.

"I am sorry, but we must distract them from the fact that you still breathe." Antonio rips my thin garment down the front, exposing me completely.

"No matter what happens," Raphael tells me, "you must be still and quiet as the dead until I tell you it is safe."

Antonio replaces the hood, lifts me in his arms, and opens the door. I make myself go completely limp. Carrying me up the stairs, he speaks to the crowd, now mostly silent.

"Here is what you came for. She is right and truly hanged. Go on about your business. Nothing left to see here." His words are met with silence. Antonio gently lays me on the boards. I feel the hood pulled off, and a cloth covers me and I am wrapped, as would be any corpse. I lay still and play my part.

"Stay still, no matter," whispers Antonio, leaning close to wrap the shroud tight. I am lifted, carried a distance and placed down. Someone pulls back the cloth around my face and I hear Raphael sobbing, but I do not open my eyes. He holds me and kisses my lips; I keep my eyes closed and do not move a muscle. He lays me down gently. I hear the scraping of wood against wood and feel my breath against something. I dare to open my eyes the smallest bit, but there is no light. The lid has been placed on my coffin.

I hear Raphael's voice. "Can we take the body, now? Surely she is no longer any danger to the Republic."

"It would save us the trouble, but I must get permission." replies a gruff voice.

The box moves. It's carried a short distance, then set down.

I hear nothing. I am alone somewhere in my coffin. I am grateful for the roughhewn nature of the box. The lid fits poorly and I can see light all around it so I may breathe. The wood is rough against my skin, but I am safe.

Time passes as I lay thanking the Almighty God for still being able to draw breath and for my angels who made this happen. Though I am grateful to be alive, I cannot help but wish myself back in the comfort of my cell. Certainly, anyone would prefer a jail cell to a coffin.

Falling asleep somehow, I awake to men's voices.

"You guard the door," I hear Raphael say to someone. Cool air as if the lid had been lifted. "You are safe, my love." Opening my eyes, I see the face I love above all others. He takes me in his arms and whispers against my ear. "I'm sorry it is taking so long. They will not agree to release you to us and insist on your speedy burial in the ground reserved for criminals. The maestro is appealing to his uncle, the cardinal, for special permission once again."

He lifts me out of the box. I find I am in a shed piled high with bales of hay. "You must stay in there a while longer, but I have brought some water and a bit of bread. Make haste to relieve yourself. I need you back in that box as soon as possible.

"What is all the commotion outside?" I ask, peaking around the bales as I hold up the shredded shift.

"Some of the people gathered to watch the hanging begged for mercy and when none was granted, they charged the gallows. The soldiers ran in to the crowd with swords drawn. I saw someone carried away and watched the soldiers wipe blood from their blades."

I remember the three in the front row who listened so intently and even provided what comfort they could. I remember the shouting as I dropped.

"Several of the soldiers were injured and there is a search for the instigators. It seems a milk maid hit a soldier over the head with a bucket, and others joined in the attack. Hurry. We must not be discovered or we will all end up in boxes."

I hurry back to stand beside Raphael and he lifts me into the box, hands me the bread and a skin of water, kisses me and replaces the lid. I say a prayer for Bess, Marco, and little Spud, who had come to matter to me as they listened to my tale and gave me comfort.

My needs attended, I fall asleep secure in the knowledge that Raphael would take care of me. But it was Tomaso Terra's face I see when next the coffin lid is again lifted off—how many hours later I cannot say. I feel painfully aware that I wear only a white muslin garment ripped down the front, leaving little covered. Tomaso's face is warm and reassuring without a trace of leering, and he hands me a small bundle.

"You must stay in there a while longer. I'm afraid we have yet to make arrangements to move the body…I mean you." He helps me out of the box, keeping his eyes averted. I hurry to see to my comfort and quickly climb back in with Tomaso's help. I am grateful for Tomaso's genteel behavior. Just as I thought he had changed, he reaches in to the box, lifts me and plants a kiss on my lips that was not the least bit brotherly. The lid closes.

I opened the bundle to find a piece of cold mutton and some cheese. Finishing the small meal, I doze off once more. I awaken to shouts that sound just outside the door. I feel the box lifted and carried, only to be set down again in but a minute.

"We must go now. Soldiers are on their way." The loud, commanding voice sounds like Raphael's, though I had never heard him speak in such a manner. But I had never spent time in a coffin, either. If soldiers come and take me, would I not be buried alive? My heart pounds as I feel the box move with the rhythm of a cart to the sound of hoof beats.

I settle down. I do not believe I had been rescued to end by suffocating in a coffin. I cannot tell how long I travel, for I fall mercifully asleep once more. I awake when the motion of the cart grows rough and my box and I slide back and forth. I hear the driver whip the horses.

Suddenly, all movement stops. The lid is lifted and I take the risk to open my eyes and look around. I am in a large barn full of horses and wagons, but I see no one. I hear Raphael outside the barn's door, yelling at someone. "You will take her over my dead body." And then I hear scuffling and grunts as if men are fighting. I lay still with my eyes closed.

Tomaso's face appears, and he puts his fingers to his lips and lifts me out of the coffin. Setting me down behind a bale of hay, I watch as he fills the coffin from burlap bags of rocks. He throws in a small, evil-smelling bundle and quickly nails the lid shut. I hear the door burst open and I move back into the shadows.

Raphael runs in dirty and bleeding and throws himself on the wooden box. "Please! You cannot take her. We were to be married. You must let me bury her in my family's churchyard."

A burly soldier raises his sword above Raphael and my heart stops. "This body is to be buried by order of the Doge in the ground for criminals and lost souls. Ain't no murderess fit for hallowed ground." The man lowers his sword as Tomaso appears and pulls Raphael away from the now stinking box of rocks.

"Come along, brother. There is nothing more we can do."

The soldier replaces his sword in its scabbard and calls to another waiting outside. Another soldier enters and the two bend to pick up the coffin. "Well, we better get this in the ground soon, by the smell of it." The burly soldier stops to wrap a kerchief around his face and bends to pick up the box.

Raphael waits until the soldiers have loaded the coffin on to a cart and the hoof beats fade away before he stops wailing. He runs to me and holds me tight. His breath soft against my ear, he says, "It is over, my love." He kisses me, then says, "The fish heads and chicken entrails will certainly discourage any opening of the box. In the morning they will likely bury that coffin, and you will be officially dead."

I am not quite sure this should make me happy, but Raphael's joy convinces me it must be so. I had, after all, survived my hanging. I could finally breathe easily again. He held me for a minute and his face grew sober. Not two feet away stands Tomaso Terra, beaming in triumph. Raphael picks me up and places me in Tomaso's arms like a bundle of rags.

"Here, Tomaso, I am a man of my word. I promised that if with your help, Gabriella lived, I would pay the price you asked. Please treat her well," said Raphael.

Tomaso received his prize carefully. He kissed me. I pushed him away, and he set me down gently. I had nearly hanged and after riding for hours in a coffin, this was more than I can bear.

"I will decide what becomes of me! I am not some object to be bartered! I turn to Raphael. "You asked me to marry you, and you will not get out of that promise by giving me to Tomaso!"

"Of course not, my love. I had another plan to steal you back before Signore Terra reduced your value too greatly."

The door opens and I jump, but it is Maestro Vivaldi. I run to him. "Oh, Maestro, now that you are here, my joy is complete. How can I thank you enough for your part in saving me?"

He looks care-worn and tired. "Your happiness and the fact that you are still in this world is enough. None of this would have succeeded without the help of these brave souls." He turns to the open door and I see three people shuffle in: a woman wrapped in a heavy velvet cloak, a man with a hood pulled down over his face and a figure as small as a child. They throw off their wraps and now my joy really is complete.

I run to them and embrace each in turn. Bess's face is bruised, and there is dried blood in her red hair. Marco smiles at me beneath two black eyes. His arm is in a sling. Beneath Spud's cloak, I see his face is pale. His head is wrapped in a bandage and there are bandages wrapped around his little body. He still wears the brown cap, though the ostrich feather now hangs bent and dirty.

The maestro places his hand on Marco's shoulder. "You may owe them your life."

"Afff," says Bess. "Weren't nothin'. I seen a lot of hangin's in my time, but I ain't and never will stand by to see no innocent girl hang."

"She threw her bucket right at the biggest soldier," says Marco.

She pulls herself up straight and goes on with the story. "And when they tried to grab me, Marco laid into 'em with big fists flyin'. Then one of 'em pulls out his sword and runs at us, and little Spud here flies around behind 'im and hits 'im square in the back of his knees. He fell flat on his face in the mud."

Marco reaches over, patting Spud on the head. "Brave little muckraker, no bigger than a minute. Then the people runs forward and there's shoutin' and pushin'. Bess and I grabs Spud and we run off into the trees. This gentleman," he points at the maestro, "offers us a ride in his wagon and here we are. We come out just fine."

I kneel down, eye to eye with the little man, and kiss him on both cheeks. He blushes bright red beneath the dirt and dried blood.

"Will he be alright?" I ask the maestro.

"The doctor said his wounds are not deep and he should recover. The brawl they started kept the soldiers from paying much attention to anything and allowed us to make off with you." The maestro beamed down at Spud.

I suddenly remember the hangman and turned to Raphael. "Was the hangman really Antonio, the stable boy from my former home?"

"Yes, he was a most important part of our little scheme. Did you not wonder why it took so long for the hangman to arrive?

"I did, but I was ever grateful for the time," I replied. "The time allowed me to make some valuable new friends."

Raphael continued his story. "In all our planning I found my brother, Anton, quite by chance, I believe you know him as Antonio. Explaining our mission, he was happy to be of assistance. We waylaid the real hangman and Antonio took his place. He replaced the short and deadly rope with a nice long one, giving you plenty of rope to reach the ground below the gallows. It seems he has fond memories of you and was sorry not to get to say goodbye." I blush crimson and Raphael laughs.

I am grateful for all of their help, but I cannot help but worry about the fate of my three new friends. "What will become of them? They cannot go back. Surely the Doge's soldiers are after them."

The maestro puts his hand on Marco's shoulder. "I think the Smithy at the Oespedale will soon be short an overseer and could use a good smith. I am certain our dairy could make use of a lady good with milk cows as well."

"A lady?" says Bess, her eyes round with surprise.

"Courage like yours, Bess, can't be found in common folk." I wrap my arms around her. "I am sorry you must leave your homes and families, but at least you won't be hanged for rioting."

Bess drew herself up, full of pride once again. "Ain't nothin' much to leave. My Louis died two years ago, and we were never blessed with children. I'm guessin' the master can always get another girl to milk his cows."

Marco stood looking at the ground in front of him.

"And you, Marco?" I ask him.

"I had thought to court a village girl named Sophie when I'd saved up enough for a wife." He did not raise his eyes.

Raphael walks over, placing his hand on Marco's broad shoulder. "If it's suitable girls to wed you are after, the best place of all is the Oespedale. That's where I found this one." He wraps his free arm around me.

The cloud seems to lift from Marco's face and only Spud stands forlornly looking at the straw covered ground. I drop down to his level once again. "Spud, I would be honored to make certain such a brave man recovers completely by taking care of him myself. I do not know where we will end up, but I know there will be a place for you in our household…if you would like."

A smile splits his face; he does a little hop and then winces with the pain of his wounds.

CHAPTER TWENTY-SIX

I escaped my hanging but my friends and I are far from safe. The soldiers will certainly be looking for those who started the riot, and if I were seen and recognized, we might all still lose our lives on the gallows. The weighted box, stinking with entrails, might fool the soldiers for a while and then again, it might not.

We formulate a plan. Tomaso provides a wagon to return the maestro, Bess, and Marco to the Ospedale. After goodbyes and thank-yous that must last a lifetime, Spud, Raphael and I set off to the north in another gift from Tomaso, a large and comfortable coach.

After changing into a silk gown, most likely meant for Tomaso's mistress as it hardly fits me, I settle down into the luxurious velvet cushions nearly as happy as I am exhausted. The wild jolting of the carriage wakes me some hours later. It is dark now. My future husband is placing something over my face. "I'm sorry, Gabriella. You need to wear this. I will explain later." This hood is made of black lace, and though it hides my face, I can see through it clearly. I wonder if wearing hoods might forever be my fate.

Raphael has changed into a handsome dove grey suit and burgundy waistcoat. The long silver lace at his neck and cuffs gives him a look I have never seen on him before.

The coach stops. Raphael puts his finger to his lips to signal Spud and uses his cloak to cover the dwarf completely.

The coach door opens. The hired driver's lips are pressed together in a hard line. He lets down the little step. Raphael winks at me and steps down, closing the coach door behind him.

"Hello there, gentle sirs," says Raphael. I see by the light of several torches a line of men in the red livery of the Doge of Venice, a dozen men on foot and at least as many on horseback. Raphael puts his hand on his hip and cocks his head. "Tell me, sirs, what pleasures do you seek?"

A man with gold braid on his shoulders opens the carriage door and the smoke from the torch he carries chokes me. I hold my breath and bow my head. Spud does not move a muscle.

"I'm sorry, sir," says Raphael to the man examining us. "In days past my mistress would have been more than happy to see to the entire company's pleasure, but now, sadly," he drops his voice to a whisper, "she suffers from the pox." There is an odd lilt in his voice. "Please let me know if there is any way I may be of service to such brave and handsome gentlemen," I hear him say.

"Ain't nothing but some poxy baud and her fancy man. Let's head back to the east. They must have slipped past us," the man says and as he closes the carriage door.

I watch through the window as Raphael takes a lace handkerchief from his pocket and waves good ye to the soldiers. I cannot help myself, I begin to laugh. As the last of the Doge's men disappear into the darkness. Raphael climbs back into the carriage.

"It is not often that I can use my upbringing as the son of a courtesan to save the life of the woman I love. That veil you wear was to be delivered to my mother, but she died before she could make use of it. The French pox took her beauty before it took her life and she would not appear in public unless veiled."

I caught my breath. "You would make a fine actor. I am certain some of the lonely soldiers cursed their captain for taking them away from such a pretty and willing fancy man." He slid across the seat and took me in his arms as the coachman whipped the horses and the coach took off again.

"You may laugh, my love. I was but mimicking the ways of my mother's man Albert. A good courtesan could provide any pleasure a man should desire."

I kiss him as a reward for his life-saving play acting.

"Are you all right, Spud? Raphael asks. He expects no answer from the mute, but there is no movement at all from the little man.

I pull back the cloak to see Spud's eyes closed, his forehead burns with fever. "We must stop somewhere and get this little hero a proper doctor," I say.

"I'm afraid there is little on this road for hours. We may find a farm and someone who can help." Raphael called to the coachman to stop. I could hear them talking and I reach for the skin of water. Having nothing else, I tear a piece from the hem of my shift and wet it to bathe Spud's forehead. But he does not stir.

We ride on for hours. I continue to bathe Spud with cool water and drip a few drops between his bone dry lips. I see that the bandage around his head is dry, but when I reach beneath the cloak to check those around his body, my hand comes away wet with his warm blood.

"We must stop now! He will die without treatment. His wounds are bleeding again," I plead. After another hour, we spy a farmhouse lit by the light of a single lantern. We stop, and Raphael alights to talk with the farmer, who is wearing a nightshirt. I expect him to play my fancy man again, but when he speaks, it is with his own voice.

"This man is badly hurt. If you could let us tend him, we would be very grateful."

The man squints at us. "You can tend him in the barn but be quiet about it. My six children don't need up at this hour." He cocks his head and looks at me. "My wife needs her sleep, too. She'll birth me another any day." He points the way to the barn and dumps a bucket of scraps to three fat piglets in a pen.

Raphael gently lifts Spud and carries him into the barn next to the pig pen. He lays him on a bale of straw as a milk cow looks on and chickens cluck. Spud is pale and still. Kneeling beside him, I open the cloak, peel back his filthy shirt, and examine the wound. It looks not deep but angry, red and hot to the touch. I peel off the dirty bandages. A young girl in a ragged gown with red hair and wide eyes, joins us.

"I seen wounds go bad like that before," she says. "Needs a poultice, he does."

"Please." I say. "Anything you can do to help. This dear little man is terribly brave and I cannot let him die." The girl disappears. I tear more strips of my shift and Raphael brings clean water from the well to clean Spud's chest. There is no soap, but I pray removing the dirt and dried blood will have to be enough. The girl returns and, without a word, applies a poultice of moss and herbs to Spud's wounds. She brings clean bandages, some rags, and a blanket. I am grateful, as my shift is nearly gone.

When we have done what we could for Spud, the girl disappears again and Raphael and I lie down on the straw bales next to him. Raphael's strong arms enfold me, and I rest my head on his chest.

A rooster crows above my head. The day has dawned. I sit up and remember that I am safe and Spud is not. When I lay my hand on his head, I find him still burning with fever. Raphael is nowhere to be found, and I search for water with which to cool my little friend's fever. Filling a bucket from the pump outside the barn, I wet some of the rags the girl left and gently swab his head. Raphael returns with a tall man in work clothes. I recognize the farmer from last night.

"Good morning, love. Mr. Correlli has just been delivered of a fine strong son. How is our patient?" He kisses me on my head and kneels beside me.

"He is no better. I do not think we should leave at least until his fever breaks."

"I am grateful for the help with the birthin'," the farmer says. "I'd be willin' to feed you and change out your horses, but I can't be puttin' my family to risk. If the Doge's men are after you like this one says, I can't take the risk of keeping you here for long."

I am worried about Spud, but I do not wish to put these kind people in any danger for helping us.

"Maybe if we travel slowly…" I say.

Raphael helps me up. "It is not more than a day's ride now. We must take the chance."

The red-haired girl returns with two large baskets of food. She kneels beside Spud, gently removes the bandages and places a new poultice on his chest. "It ain't bleedin' no more. That's a good sign and the oozin' is clear." She sits back on her heels and looks at me. "Who is the little fellow anyways?"

"He is someone courageous who risked himself to try and save me."

The girl looks at me with narrowed eyes. "Looks like he done his job, then." She rose and was out the barn door without another word.

Raphael wakes the coachman, who is still sleeping in the coach, and they carry Spud as gently as possible. I follow with the baskets of food. "We are grateful for all your help," I say to another girl who comes around the side of the barn.

This one has long brown hair in braids, and her wide smile reveals dimples in both cheeks. "My mama is grateful for his help. She's had trouble with these last two births. My pa ain't no good at helpin'. Seems the gentleman knew just what to do." She gives me a nod. There is still much I do not know about this man dressed in silver lace with wild curls upon his head.

Raphael joins me in the carriage, and we eat a fine breakfast from the generous food in the baskets. There is fresh bread, butter and jam, a whole cheese, a roast chicken and apples. He then climbs up to ride with the driver again and the coach rolls on much more slowly than before, but the road is thin and rough. Spud is so still I have to touch him to make sure he still breathes. The fever lets me know he is still alive.

The coach stops and Raphael gets into the carriage. He had been riding up with the coachman to make sure Spud could lie flat and had room to rest well. I am glad of his company again. He kisses me briefly and I answer his unspoken question about Spud's condition with a shake of my head.

"He will get better when he can rest. We will soon be there," says Raphael.

"Where is there?" I ask.

Raphael gives me a smile and answers, "You will see soon enough."

"How did you know to help the farmer's wife with her birthing?" I ask.

"As for the farmer's wife, I have always helped with the livestock births and it was not a different one, really."

We ride on for several hours more. At last, the coach stops. Raphael sticks his head out the coach window and then turns to me. "We are home." He opens the coach door, pulls out the little steps and helps me down.

Before us, I see a lovely white stone house on a hill overlooking the sea. The house has two stories and eight windows across the front. The property includes a large barn and several outbuildings. At the bottom of the hill is a long dock, with two small boats and a barge tied up to it.

"Oh, Raphael, this is beautiful." I wrap my arms around him.

With his lips against mine, he says, "Where else would I have you spend your life with me? I cannot have you regret that you are not Tomaso Terra's favorite mistress."

I climb back into the coach and when I place my hand on Spud's forehead, I find it cool. His eyelids flutter and his eyes open. My happiness is complete.

EPILOGUE

We were married a week later. Raphael assured me our home was far enough from Venice that we would not be bothered by the Doge, who cares less for justice than for the gold he receives as bribes.

My husband and I worked tirelessly, and his import business has made us wealthy. I often wondered as I helped him examine a load of velvets from the orient, if some of it would go to my father's factory near Florence to be embellished. I would wonder if some of it might be made into a suit for Tomaso's son or a gown for his mistress. Or even if some of that fine velvet might become trim on the maestro's Easter vestments.

God has blessed us with six children, two sets of twin boys and two girls. Though it might have been unwise to be seen in my former home, it was by far one of the most joyous days in my life to introduce my oldest sons to their uncles and namesakes, Roberto and Richardo, on my sons' tenth birthday. It was a rare day I dared to travel to my home and it was indeed worth the risk.

I managed to see my mother and father several times more until they became too old to travel. They now rest in heaven with my first babe. I hope my mother gives comfort to the little boy who never got to know this world but will always have a piece of my heart.

One of the greatest gifts in my life has been the wonderful friends I have been blessed with. I feel so fortunate to have had the company of Spud these long years. Though we never knew how old he was, I enjoyed his company for forty years. I would never allow such a brave and talented man to clean my stalls but was grateful to have his help teaching music to my children. After all, I would never presume to teach anyone the violin, but it is far too lovely an instrument to deny them.

My daughters benefitted greatly from his instruction. Raphaella became a virtuoso and played with a grand orchestra until she ran off to marry an actor. Even my younger girl, Angelina, learned to play works I could never do justice to. I encouraged the boys as well, but all four took more interest in learning their father's business than in music lessons I insisted they take.

When my children grew up and had children of their own, Spud taught them, too. There came a day when Spud came to sit in his little rocking chair by the fire in our kitchen, as he did each evening after dinner. That evening, when he did not rise to go to his room as usual, I covered him with a blanket, kissed his head and bade him rest well. In the morning, he sat still and cold. My little friend, hero and cherished teacher was gone.

It took several years, but I did see the maestro again after my hanging, and he brought me the most beautiful gift: four lovely violin concerti that would come to be known as "The Four Seasons." I have to admit, the movement called "Winter" is my favorite, for though each season is lovely for its calm and its storms, the genius of the maestro is so apparent in this movement. I still shed tears for the tragic and beautiful girl that inspired "Winter". I do love the "Summer" movement and I am proud if I provided some small inspiration.

I am very old now, grown weary to the marrow of my bones. Each night that I close my eyes may truly be my last. Before I go to sleep, every night my last thoughts are of one of my loves. It is not my first Antonio, who awakened my desire and played such a vital part in saving my life. It is not Tomaso, whom I cannot think of even now without a little longing where it should not be.

He helped me remember the joy of life while I was imprisoned. Without his help, I would surely have died. Though I will always love him, he rarely arouses more than a wistful smile on my ancient lips.

I do not think of my dearest love, Raphael, when I close my eyes at night, though he fills my thoughts nearly every minute of every day. I love this wonderful man with whom I have spent my life and who now lies sleeping beside me. He loved me enough to offer me to another in exchange for my life. I love him for the genius of his intricate plans that saved me and made us a wonderful life. I love him for all that he is. His curls are just as wild, though now white, and his eyes are just as blue. He is the love of my life and forever owns my heart.

And yet, shamefully, it is not my Raphael I think of last each night.

I have honestly shared my feelings in each word of this story. Now I must make this final confession. Every night before I fall asleep, I think only of him: the genius whose music has thrilled the world with its beauty and its joy. The music my children and I have played ten thousand times. My hands grow stiff with the years and I can hardly do his works justice, but I play at least one each day on my piano or hautboy—oboe, as they call it now. I fall asleep every night, be it my last or no, thinking of the love of my musician's soul, Antonio Vivaldi, The Maestro.

THE END

Don't miss out on your next favorite book!

Join the Satin Romance mailing list
www.satinromance.com/mail.html

THANK YOU FOR READING

Did you enjoy this book?

We invite you to leave a review at your favorite book site, such as Goodreads, Amazon, Barnes & Noble, etc.

DID YOU KNOW THAT LEAVING A REVIEW…

- Helps other readers find books they may enjoy.
- Gives you a chance to let your voice be heard.
- Gives authors recognition for their hard work.
- Doesn't have to be long. A sentence or two about why you liked the book will do.

ABOUT THE AUTHOR

 As a little girl, Melissa Rea would fall asleep whispering stories to herself in the dark. She got in to trouble in elementary school for embellishing when the truth just seemed too mundane. She grew up and the stories became just daydreams and she pursued a sensible career. Melissa filled her spare time with the wondrous worlds of Bram Stoker, Mary Shelly, Robert Heinlein, Philippa Gregory, Stephen King, Dean Koontz, Jackie Collins, Jennifer Weiner, Sarah Dunant and any and all authors who caught her fancy. And still, the stories in her head were there, now influenced by the delicious words of others. One day, the stories could no longer be contained, and she began to write novels. *Conjuring Casanova* was published in 2016 and was a Recommended Indie Book by Kirkus Review. It won first place in the Beverly Hills International Book Awards for Romantic Comedy, a first place in ReadersViews Reviewers Choice Awards for Romance and was a finalist in Forward Reviews Book of the Year in the Romance category. She lives in St. Louis where she has a solo dental practice and lives with her husband and rescue cats.

www.facebook.com/melissareaauthor